EGE
RY

D1393420

dr

Oliver Twist

or befc

by

CHARLES DICKENS

arranged as a play in two acts by

Guy Williams

WITHDRAWN

Nelson

105128
Aberdeen College Library

Thomas Nelson and Sons Ltd
Nelson House Mayfield Road
Walton-on-Thames Surrey
KT12 5PL UK

Nelson Blackie
Wester Cleddens Road
Bishopbriggs
Glasgow G64 2NZ UK

Thomas Nelson Australia
102 Dodds Street
South Melbourne
Victoria 3205 Australia

Nelson Canada
1120 Birchmount Road
Scarborough Ontario
M1K 5G4 Canada

© Guy Williams 1969

First published by Macmillan Education Ltd 1969
ISBN 0-333-06781-9

This edition published by Thomas Nelson and Sons Ltd 1992

I(T)P Thomas Nelson is an International
Thomson Publishing Company

I(T)P is used under licence
ISBN 0-17-432464-2
NPN 9 8 7 6 5

All rights reserved. No part of this publication may be
reproduced, copied or transmitted save with written permission or
in accordance with the provisions of the Copyright, Design and
Patents Act 1988, or under the terms of any licence permitting
limited copying issued by the Copyright Licensing Agency,
90 Tottenham Court Road, London W1P 9HE.

Any person who does any unauthorised act in relation to
this publication may be liable to criminal prosecution and civil
claims for damages.

For permission to perform this play, application must be made
to Thomas Nelson and Sons Ltd, unless no charge is being made.

Printed in Singapore

FOREWORD

DRAMASCRIPTS are intended for use in secondary schools, amateur theatrical groups and youth clubs. The plays range widely from established classics to new works and adaptations of books and film scripts. There is nothing in any of the plays that is beyond the capabilities of younger actors. They may be used in a variety of ways: read privately for pleasure or aloud in groups, acted in the classroom, church hall or youth club, or in public performances.

With OLIVER TWIST, Charles Dickens captured the imagination of the world - no other story has been more consistently loved than that of the little orphan boy who was kept on starvation rations in a parish work-house, and who dared to ask for more. This dramatisation contains that famous scene, and many others. In it, we meet Fagin and his irrepressible gang of young thieves; the pompous bully Mr Bumble and the arch Mrs Corney, by whom the Beadle is effectively bullied; the murderous Bill Sikes and his moll Nancy, whom he does to death; and several other unforgettable characters. The play ends with one of the most gruesome 'execution scenes' that have ever been written. Definitely not for the chicken-hearted, this one - but the very greatest fun for everybody else.

GUY WILLIAMS
Advisory Editor

OLIVER TWIST

This shortened version of *Oliver Twist* was originally prepared for a special purpose—to be acted by the dramatic society of an old grammar school, in a bare assembly hall with a flat, raised, uncurtained platform at one end.

In these apparently unpromising conditions the society has performed in recent years a number of the most notable English plays, finding that changes of scene can be quite adequately suggested by the turning of a screen, by a change in lighting, or by the addition or subtraction of some portable property, such as a chair, a joint-stool, or an improvised pillory.

It is not easy to condense a story as complex and colourful as *Oliver Twist* into two acts that can be sat through with pleasure by a present-day audience, and inevitably the shears have had to be used rather harshly. Wherever possible, the text of the 1880 Pocket Volume edition (published by Chapman and Hall) has been adhered to. The extensions of the text were made necessary by the requirements of scene-changing.

Parmiter's, 1969   G.R.W.

PRODUCTION NOTES

The scenes between Mr. Bumble and Mrs. Corney in Act Two can be played, where conditions permit, on a substage or apron stage, the transitions to the Infirmary and back being effected by changes of lighting.

Nancy's last speeches have been left as far as possible in Dickens's own words. They should be shortened or altered if they prove too difficult for the actress to sustain in their present form.

The murder of Nancy may be presented very effectively by plotting a complete blackout after

'... time. A little, little time!'

Then the stage can remain in total darkness to the end of the scene, except for a brief lightning flash at

'Mercy, Lord, have mercy ...'

The newsboy can be used to attract the attention of the audience from the stage.

THE CHARACTERS

OLIVER TWIST, a young man looking back at his childhood.
MR. LIMBKINS, Chairman of the Workhouse Board
OTHER MEMBERS OF THE BOARD
MR. SLOUT, the Master of the Workhouse
MR. BUMBLE, a parish beadle
MRS. CORNEY, the Matron of the Workhouse
YOUNG OLIVER
A TALL PAUPER
A THIN PAUPER
MR. SOWERBERRY, a parochial undertaker
MRS. SOWERBERRY, his wife
NOAH CLAYPOLE, a charity boy, apprenticed to Mr. Sowerberry
CHARLOTTE, a servant to Mrs. Sowerberry
JOHN DAWKINS ('THE ARTFUL DODGER'), a young pickpocket
FAGIN, a receiver of stolen goods
CHARLEY BATES, a thief, one of Fagin's apprentices
CHITLING, a thief
KAGS, a thief
BILL SIKES, a brutal thief and housebreaker
NANCY, Sikes' mistress
MONKS, a half-brother of Oliver Twist
MR. BROWNLOW, a benevolent old gentleman
MRS. BEDWIN, his housekeeper
MR. GRIMWIG, his friend
A FEMALE PAUPER
OLD SALLY, a workhouse inmate
AN OLD WOMAN, attendant in the Infirmary
AN APOTHECARY'S APPRENTICE
TOBY CRACKIT, a housebreaker
With: PAUPERS, CITIZENS and PRISON OFFICIALS

ACT ONE

SCENE ONE
THE PARISH WORKHOUSE

(Oliver enters)

Oliver. Have you ever been hungry? So hungry that you haven't been able to do anything but think about your stomach? And how you are going to fill it? I've been like that for weeks and months at a time. You see, I was born at a Charity Workhouse, where my mother had been taken in an exhausted state. She had been found lying in the street the previous night, having walked a great distance, for her shoes were worn to pieces. She died, poor thing, when I was a few minutes old. I was brought up by the worthy Members of the Board of Guardians . . .

(The Members of the Board enter, with **Mr. Slout,** *the Master of the Workhouse. They sit down at an official table, to one side.)*

. . . and by their Beadle, Mr. Bumble . . .

*(***Mr. Bumble*** *enters, and bows to the Board.)*

. . . This is Mrs. Corney, the Matron of the Workhouse . . .

*(***Mrs. Corney*** *enters, and curtseys to Mr. Bumble.)*

. . . When I was eight or ten months old, the Members of the Board decided that I should be farmed out, and I was sent to a small Branch Workhouse some three miles off. But the time soon came when they wanted me back.

Mr. Bumble. I shall be away for a few hours, Mrs. Corney, upon porochial business connected with the porochial orphans . . .

*(***Mrs. Corney*** *inclines her head.)*

. . . The child that was half-baptized Oliver Twist is nine year old today.

Mrs. Corney. Bless him!

Mr. Bumble. And notwithstanding an offered reward of ten pound,

1

which was afterwards increased to twenty pound. Notwithstanding the most superlative, and, I may say, supernat'ral exertions on the part of this parish, we have never been able to discover who is his father, or what was his mother's settlement, name, or con—dition.

Mrs. Corney *(Raising her hands in astonishment).* How does he come to have any name at all, then?

Mr. Bumble *(Drawing himself up with great pride).* I inwented it.

Mrs. Corney. You, Mr. Bumble!

Mr. Bumble. I, Mrs. Corney. We names our foundlings in alphabetical order. The last was an S,—Swubble, I named him. This was a T,—Twist, I named him. The next one as comes will be Unwin, and the next Vilkins. I have got names ready made to the end of the alphabet, and all the way through it again, when we come to Z.

Mrs. Corney. Why, you're quite a literary character, Sir!

Mr. Bumble *(Evidently gratified).* Well, well, perhaps I may be. Perhaps I may be, Mrs. Corney. Oliver being now too old to remain at the Branch Workhouse, the Board 'as determined to have him back here. I am going out myself to fetch him, as the porochial delegate, the porochial stipendiary. I will see him at once.

*(*Mr. Bumble *picks up his porochial cane and goes out.* Mrs. Corney *goes to a large copper, and stirs.)*

The Chairman of the Board. The intentions of the Poor Law Acts were undoubtedly good, Gentlemen, but alas! the poor people don't seem to mind coming to our Workhouse. Unless we are very careful, our Workhouse may become a regular place of public entertainment for the poorer classes; a tavern, where there is nothing to pay; a public breakfast, dinner, tea and supper all the year round; a brick and mortar elysium, where it is all play and no work!

Other Members of the Board. Hear! Hear! It's disgraceful! It's a scandal!

The Chairman. But we are the fellows to set this to rights. We'll stop it in no time. We must establish this rule: that all poor people shall have an alternative. We'll compel nobody, not us. They shall have the alternative of being starved by a gradual process in the house, or by a quick one out of it. Are we agreed on that, Gentlemen? . . .

(General agreement.)

. . . Mrs. Corney! . . .

*(***Mrs. Corney*** *stops stirring and goes to curtsey to the Board.)*

. . . Mrs. Corney, we have contracted with the waterworks to lay on an unlimited supply of water. We have contracted with a corn factor to supply periodically certain quantities—certain small quantities—of oatmeal. We have instructed dear Mr. Slout to issue three meals of thin gruel only per day. You may give the paupers one onion each, Mrs. Corney, twice a week, and as a treat half a roll on Sundays. Do you understand, Mrs. Corney? There's no saying how many applicants for parochial assistance may not start up in all classes of society if we don't look ahead. We must make relief inseparable from the Workhouse, and from gruel. That'll frighten people.

*(***Mr. Bumble*** *appears, with* **Young Oliver.***)*

Young Oliver. Are we nearly there?

Mr. Bumble. Nearly there? We're there. Now just you smarten yourself up, me boy. It's a Board night, and the Board has said that you are to appear before it forthwith . . .

(He taps Oliver with his porochial cane.)

. . . So wake yourself up . . .

(He taps Oliver again.)

. . . And make yourself lively. And follow me.

*(***Mr. Bumble*** *takes Oliver before the Board.)*

. . . Bow to the Board, Oliver.

Oliver. Seeing no Board but the table, I bowed to that.

The Chairman. What's your name, boy?

*(***Young Oliver*** *trembles.* **Mr. Bumble** *gives him another tap behind, which makes him cry out.)*

A Member in a White Waistcoat. The boy's a fool.

The Chairman. Boy, listen to me. You know you're an orphan, I suppose?

Young Oliver. What's that, sir?

The Member in the White Waistcoat. The boy is a fool—I thought he was.

3

The Chairman. Hush! *(To Young Oliver.)* You know you've got no father or mother, and that you were brought up by the parish, don't you?

Young Oliver *(Weeping).* Yes, sir.

The Member in the White Waistcoat. What can the boy be crying for?

A Third Member. I hope you say your prayers every night and pray for the people who feed you, and take care of you, like a Christian?

Young Oliver. Yes, sir.

The Chairman. Well! You have come here to be educated, and taught a useful trade . . .

The Member in the White Waistcoat. So you'll begin to pick oakum tomorrow morning at six o'clock.

The Chairman. Take him away, Mr. Bumble . . .

(Mr. Bumble leads Young Oliver aside.)

. . . Well, Gentlemen, I think that concludes our formal business, so if you would care to join me in a glass of the parish's wine, I think we may adjourn.

(The Chairman signals to Mr. Slout. **The Master of the Workhouse** *pours wine for* **The Members of the Board**, *who move off, with their glasses, to a not-far-distant place. As they do so,* **the Pauper Children** *who have been sitting round the stage move up with their bowls and spoons towards the copper.* **Mr. Slout** *gives* **Young Oliver** *a bowl and a spoon and puts him at the very end of a bench.* **Mrs. Corney** *ladles a little gruel into each bowl.)*

Mrs. Corney. Shall you say Grace, Mr. Slout?

Mr. Slout. Silence, please, paupers. For what the Good Lord and the kind Board of Guardians have seen fit to give us to eat, let each and every one of us be thankful. You may begin . . .

(The Paupers eat ravenously, and then sit staring at the copper as if they would like to devour the very bricks of which it is composed.)

. . . And now, Mrs. Corney, our own meals await us, I believe, in our own quarters.

(Mr. Slout and Mrs. Corney go, Mrs. Corney sniffing and observing 'smells good!' as she leaves the stage. Mr. Bumble, attendant upon the Board, is unaware of the paupers. Their

4

attention is still fixed on the empty copper.)

Oliver. For my first six months in the Main Workhouse, this system was in full operation. It was rather expensive at first, in consequence of the increase in the undertaker's bill, and the necessity of taking in the clothes of all the paupers, which fluttered loosely on our wasted, shrunken forms after a week or two's gruel. But the number of workhouse inmates got thin as well as the paupers; and the board were in ecstacies.

At last, we became wild with hunger. There was one boy among us, tall for his age . . .

(The Tall Pauper stands up.)

. . . who hadn't been used to that sort of thing, for his father had kept a small cookshop.

The Tall Pauper. It's not right, I tell yer. It's not right. I gets so 'ungry I could just about eat the cove sleeping next to me, these nights . . .

(There is a grim chuckle.)

. . . You can laugh! You'll laugh on the other side of your fices if wakes up one morning and find I've 'ad your leg off. I will, too, if they don't give me another basin of gruel every day. I'll stop at nothing when I gets desperate!

A Thin Pauper *(Standing up).* Tosher's right. We're all starving to death. But what are we going to do about it?

The Tall Pauper. We'll have to ask for more, that's all.

All Paupers. For more? . . . But that's . . . But Mr. Bumble . . . But . . . But . . . But . . .

The Thin Pauper. That's gammon. We won't get more at all. We'll just get a taste of old Bumble's stick for our pains. We get enough stick-oil on our seats as it is, without goin' and askin' for it.

The Tall Pauper. Well, what's the alternative? Just sit here and do nothing until we've all withered away?

A Third Pauper. It's worth a try, to my way of thinking.

(Murmurs of assent.)

The Thin Pauper. But who's going to do the askin'? You goin' to do it yourself, Tosher, since you're that keen?

The Tall Pauper. Me? No. We'll draw lots. That'll be fair, won't it?

(There is absolute silence.)

... Well, won't it? ...

(Still silence.)

... Are you all afraid, or something? ...

(He looks at each of the paupers in turn. Each, under the Tall Boy's surveillance, shakes his head. Last, the Tall Boy *looks at Young Oliver. There is a moment of tension before* Young Oliver, *too, moves his head sideways.)*

... Well, we're all agreed then. Give us some straws and we'll do it now ...

(One of the boys passes some straws, from near the copper. The Tall Pauper *turns his back on the others and arranges the straws between his hands, so that the ends only protrude.)*

... There you are ...

(He turns.)

... All them straws is long but one, and I've bit that one off short. The cove what gets the short one is the one what asks for more. After supper tonight. See?

(He offers the straws round, and each of the paupers takes one in turn.)

Oliver. I knew with absolute certainty as he took the straws round that the short one was destined for me. I nearly cried out 'Why are we wasting our time like this? I'm the boy! I know I'm the boy!'

*(*The Tall Pauper *stops before Young Oliver.* Young Oliver *takes the end of one of the two remaining straws and pulls it.)*

The Tall Pauper. It's the short one!

(There are general cries of 'Oliver!' and 'Oliver Twist!' ... 'Oliver Twist to ask for more!' ... 'Oliver Twist to ask for more!' Mr. Bumble, *hearing the noise, appears and walks slowly across the stage tapping the side of his leg with the porochial cane.* The Paupers *freeze back silently in fear as he passes.)*

Oliver. The hours crept slowly by, but eventually that evening arrived, and we boys took our places near the copper.

6

(Mrs. Corney comes in, followed by Mr. Slout.)

Mrs. Corney. A lovely sirloin, Mr. Slout, with mushrooms, and all the trimmings. You never saw such a dish. The juices in that beef! You're welcome to a slice if you'd care to look in after the boys has had their supper . . .

(She goes to the copper, and distributes gruel.)

. . . Shall you say Grace, Mr. Slout?

Mr. Slout. Silence, please, paupers. For what the Good Lord, the kind Board of Guardians and the Ratepayers of this Parish have seen fit to give us to eat, let each and every one of us be thankful. You may begin . . .

(The Paupers gulp down their gruel. Then all look at Young Oliver. There are whispers and winks and even a nudge or two. At last Young Oliver stands up and walks slowly towards the copper. Mr. Slout and Mrs. Corney, still talking beef, are thus rudely interrupted.)

Young Oliver. Please, sir . . .

Mr. Slout. Yes?

Young Oliver. Please, sir, I want some more.

(Mr. Slout gazes in stupefied astonishment on the small rebel for some seconds, and then clings for support to the copper.)

Mr. Slout *(In a faint voice).* What's that?

Young Oliver. Please, sir, I . . . WANT . . . SOME . . . MORE.

Mrs. Corney *(With a loud scream).* Oh, the limb of Satan!

Mr. Slout. Fetch the Beadle! Get Mr. Bumble! Get Mr. Bumble! Oh, you ungrateful young devil!

(He grabs Mrs. Corney's ladle, and starts to belabour Young Oliver with it. Mrs. Corney hastens to Mr. Bumble.)

Mrs. Corney. Mr. Bumble! Mr. Bumble! Oliver Twist has asked for more!

Mr. Bumble. For more? That, Mrs. Corney, sounds like revolution . . .

(The Beadle needs no urging to deal with Young Oliver. Seeing that the boy has been safely pinioned by Mr. Slout, he hastens to tell the Members of the Board.)

... Mr. Limbkins! I beg your pardon, Sir! Oliver Twist has asked for more!

The Chairman. For more?

Mr. Bumble. For more, Sir. For more.

The Chairman. Gentlemen, there appears to be a crisis in the affairs of our Workhouse. Shall we adjourn to our Board? ...

*(*The Guardians *mount to the table at which they sat before.)*

... Now compose yourself, Bumble, and answer me distinctly. Do I understand that Oliver Twist asked for more after he had eaten the supper allotted by the dietary?

Mr. Bumble. He did, Sir.

The Member in the White Waistcoat. That boy will be hung. I know that boy will be hung.

(An animated discussion takes place, in which the words 'Beat him!' 'Starve him!' and 'Transportation!' are clearly heard, followed by 'Saving of expenditure!' 'Look well in the accounts!' and 'Have a printed report published!' At last the Chairman *stands up.)*

The Chairman. We are agreed, then, gentlemen. The decision of the Board, Mr. Bumble, is this: you shall take that ungrateful boy away instantly and confine him in a dark and solitary room ...

*(*Mrs. Corney *grips Young Oliver.)*

... having flogged him well first, of course, on the way ...

*(*Mr. Bumble *brandishes the porochial cane.)*

... We shall be taking some steps to see that he is no longer a charge on our parish ...

*(*One of the Board *is laboriously inscribing the words OLIVER TWIST on a large notice.)*

... In the meantime, you had better keep the brute on half rations ...

*(*Young Oliver *whimpers.)*

... and give him the stick in the dining room occasionally as a warning and example to the others...

(A cry.)

. . . Mr. Slout!

*(*Young Oliver *is marched out by* **Mrs. Corney, Mr. Bumble** *following in full porochial majesty.* **The Chairman** *hands Mr. Slout the notice.* **Mr. Slout** *shuffles away and hangs it up in a prominent position. One by one* **The Members of the Board** *go across to inspect the notice, and to nod at it with satisfaction, before they go out. The last is* **The Member in the White Waistcoat***.)*

The Member in the White Waistcoat *(Reading).* 'Five Pounds Reward. The above sum will be paid to any man or woman who wants an apprentice for any trade, business or calling who will take a boy called Oliver Twist off the hands of the parish.' I never was more convinced of anything in my life, I never was more convinced of anything in my life, than I am that that boy will come to be hung.

(The first strokes of the porochial cane can be heard off-stage as **Mr. Slout***, left alone at the Board, raises and drains dry each of the bottles of the parish's wine before he carries them back to the Workhouse pantry.)*

SCENE TWO
AT MR. SOWERBERRY'S

Oliver. I was taken, after a lot of bargaining, by the Parish undertaker, Mr. Sowerberry. It was arranged that I should go to him 'upon liking'—a phrase which means, in the case of a parish apprentice, that if the master find, upon a short trial, that he can get enough work out of a boy without putting too much food into him, he shall have him for a term of years, to do what he likes with.

Mr. Sowerberry *(Who is working on a coffin).* And why not? I pay a good deal towards the poor's rates, don't I? Haven't I the right to get as much out of them as I can? There's not much to be made, in this game. Three or four inches over one's calculation makes a great hole in one's profits: especially when one has a family to provide for.

(There is a loud rap on the door, and **Mr. Bumble** *appears in full ceremonial outdoor rig. Behind him cowers* **Young Oliver***, in a*

9

clean shirt. **Young Oliver** *is carrying all his worldly belongings in a brown paper parcel half a foot square by three inches deep.)*

Mr. Sowerberry *(Without looking round).* Aha! Is that you, Bumble?

Mr. Bumble. No one else, Mr. Sowerberry.

Mr. Sowerberry. I have taken the measure of the two women that died last night, Mr. Bumble.

Mr. Bumble. You'll make your fortune, Mr. Sowerberry . . .

(Mr. Bumble thrusts his thumb and forefinger into Mr. Sowerberry's snuffbox, which resembles a miniature coffin.)

. . . I say you'll make your fortune, Mr. Sowerberry.

Mr. Sowerberry. Think so? The prices allowed by the Board are very small, Mr. Bumble.

Mr. Bumble. So are the coffins, Mr. Sowerberry.

(Mr. Bumble allows himself as near an approach to a laugh as a great official ought to indulge in.)

Mr. Sowerberry. Well, well, Mr. Bumble, there's no denying that since the new system of feeding has come in, the coffins are narrower and more shallow than they used to be, but we must have some profit, Mr. Bumble. Well seasoned timber is an expensive article, Sir, and all the iron handles come, by canal, from Birmingham.

Mr. Bumble. Well, well, every trade has its drawbacks. A fair profit is, of course, allowable.

Mr. Sowerberry. Of course, of course. And if I don't get a profit upon this or that particular article, why, I make it up in the long run, you see—he! he! he!

Mr. Bumble. Just so. Haw! Haw! Here! I've brought the boy.

(At a signal, **Young Oliver** *makes a bow.)*

Mr. Sowerberry *(Raising a lantern above his head to get a better view of Young Oliver).* Oh, that's the boy, is it? . . .

(He calls through to a little room behind the shop.)

. . . Mrs. Sowerberry, will you have the goodness to come here a moment, my dear? . . .

(Mrs. Sowerberry emerges. She is a short, thin, squeezed up woman, with a vixenish countenance.)

. . . My dear, this is the boy from the workhouse that I told you of.

(Young Oliver bows again.)

Mrs. Sowerberry. Dear me! He's very small.

Mr. Bumble. Why, he is rather small . . .

(He looks at Young Oliver as if it is the boy's fault that he is no bigger.)

. . . He is small. There's no denying it. But he'll grow, Mrs. Sowerberry—he'll grow.

Mrs. Sowerberry. Ah, I dare say he will—on our victuals and our drink. I see no saving in parish children, not I; for they always cost more to keep than they're worth. However, men always think they know best. We'll have to do what we can with you, little bag of bones . . .

(She calls her maid servant.)

. . . Here, Charlotte, give this boy some of the cold bits that were put by for Trip. The dog hasn't come home since the morning, so he may go without 'em. I dare say the boy isn't too dainty to eat 'em—are you, boy?

Mr. Sowerberry. Perhaps you would care to step into the parlour and have a little drop of somethink before you go, Mr. Bumble? You've had a very long walk.

Mr. Bumble. Well, perhaps, just a little drop, Mr. Sowerberry, and thank you kindly.

*(**Charlotte** puts a basin marked 'DOG' on the ground in front of Young Oliver as the adults go out.)*

Mrs. Sowerberry *(Turning back).* Your bed's under the counter, boy. You don't mind sleeping among the coffins, I suppose? But it doesn't much matter whether you do or don't, for you can't ·sleep anywhere else.

Oliver. The shop was close and hot. The atmosphere seemed tainted with the smell of coffins. I was alone, with no friends to care for, and no friends to care for me . . .

(The light fades slowly as Oliver is saying this.)

. . . I wished as I crept into my narrow bed that it were my coffin, and that I could be laid in a calm and lasting sleep in the

11

churchyard ground, with the tall grass waving gently over my head and the sound of the old deep bell to soothe me in my slumber.

I was awakened, in the morning, by a loud kicking at the outside of the shop door . . .

(Daylight. **Young Oliver** *struggles into his shirt. The kicking is repeated in an angry and impetuous manner about twenty-five times.)*

Noah Claypole *(Outside).* Open the door, will yer?

Young Oliver. I will, directly, Sir.

Noah Claypole *(Through the key-hole).* I suppose yer the new boy, ain't yer?

Young Oliver. Yes, Sir.

Noah Claypole. How old are yer?

Young Oliver. Ten, Sir.

Noah Claypole. Then I'll whop yer when I get in. You just see if I don't, that's all, my work'us brat!

(He whistles, until **Young Oliver** *manages to open the door.)*

Young Oliver. I beg your pardon, Sir. Did you knock?

Noah Claypole. I kicked.

Young Oliver. Do you want a coffin, Sir?

Noah Claypole. You'll want a coffin before long, if you tries to be funny with me. Yer don't know who I am, I suppose, Work'us?

Young Oliver. No, Sir,

Noah Claypole. I'm Mister Noah Claypole and you're under me. Take down the shutters, yer idle young ruffian . . .

(He kicks Young Oliver.)

. . . and carry them through to the yard. That's yer first job. I'll find plenty more for yer afterwards . . .

*(***Young Oliver** *tries to remove the shutters. They are too heavy for him, and there is a tinkle of falling glass.)*

. . . Cor! You've broken the winder! You'll catch it when Mrs. Sowerberry gits hold on yer! 'Ere, I'll give yer a hand . . .

(Together the boys struggle out with the shutters. As they return, **Charlotte** *appears.)*

12

Charlotte. Come through to the fire, Noah. I've saved a nice little bit of bacon for you from Master's breakfast. Oliver, I've put some bits out for you on the cover of the bread-pan. There's your tea there, too. Take it away to your box . . .

Noah Claypole. To yer kennel.

Charlotte. And drink it there, and make haste, for they'll want you to mind the shop. D'ye hear?

Noah Claypole. D'ye hear, Work'us?

Charlotte. Lor, Noah! What a rum creature you are! Why don't you let the boy alone?

Noah Claypole. Let him alone! Why, everybody lets him alone enough, for the matter of that. Neither his father nor his mother will ever interfere with him. All his relations let him have his own way pretty well. Eh, Charlotte? He! he! he!

Charlotte. Oh, you queer soul! . . .

(She bursts into a hearty laugh, in which she is joined by **Noah Claypole***; after which they both look scornfully at poor Young Oliver as he sits shivering on the box in the coldest corner of the room, eating the stale pieces that have been specially reserved for him.)*

. . . Come on, Noah.

(As they go out, **Mr. Sowerberry** *can be heard offstage, singing 'The Strife is o'er, the battle won . . .' quite cheerfully. He enters, and puts on his woodworking apron.)*

Mr. Sowerberry *(Kindly).* Good morning, Oliver . . .

*(***Young Oliver** *stands up.)*

. . . No, sit down and get on with your breakfast, lad. I'll get the shop tidy, then I'll be ready to go out if any business has—h'm—materialized during the night. It's a nice sickly season, just at this time. To use a commercial phrase, Oliver, coffins is looking up.

*(***Mrs. Sowerberry** *sweeps in.)*

Mrs. Sowerberry. Ain't you finished your breakfast yet, bag o'bones? Hurry up. We want the basin for Trip.

Mr. Sowerberry. My dear—

Mrs. Sowerberry *(Sharply).* Well?

Mr. Sowerberry. Nothing, my dear, nothing.

Mrs. Sowerberry. Ugh, you brute!

Mr. Sowerberry *(Humbly).* Not at all, my dear. I thought you didn't want to hear, my dear. I was only going to say . . .

Mrs. Sowerberry. Oh, don't tell me what you were going to say. I am nobody; don't consult me, pray. I don't want to intrude upon your secrets.

(She gives an hysterical laugh, which threatens violent consequences.)

Mr. Sowerberry. But, my dear, I want to ask your advice.

Mrs. Sowerberry. No, no, don't ask mine. Ask somebody else's.

*(Another hysterical laugh, which frightens **Mr. Sowerberry** very much.)*

Mr. Sowerberry. It's only about young Twist, my dear. A very good-looking boy, that, my dear.

Mrs. Sowerberry. He need be, for he eats enough.

Mr. Sowerberry. There's an expression of melancholy in his face, my dear, which is very interesting. He would make a delightful mute, my love . . .

*(**Mrs. Sowerberry** looks at him in wonderment.)*

. . . I don't mean a regular mute to attend grown-up people, my dear, but only for children's practice. It would be very new to have a mute in proportion, my dear. You may depend upon it, it would have a superb effect.

Mrs. Sowerberry. What an obvious suggestion! Why ever didn't you think of it before?

*(**The Sowerberrys** dress Young Oliver in mourning clothes, with a black hat band that reaches down to his knees. When they have finished, **Mrs. Sowerberry** calls **Noah Claypole** and **Charlotte** to admire the results. **Charlotte** is delighted. **Noah Claypole** is jealous of the attention that is being showered on Young Oliver, and glowers at the new boy. There is a muffled knock. **Mr. Sowerberry** goes to the door and speaks to someone on the threshold.)*

Mr. Sowerberry. Who? Bayton? Dead? Good! . . . Yes, I'll be along at once . . .

14

(He speaks to Mrs. Sowerberry.)

. . . Business, dear. Sent medicine in a blacking bottle yesterday. Wouldn't take it. Gone this morning. Doesn't that show? . . .

(To Noah Claypole.)

. . . Noah, look after the shop. The sooner this job is done, the better.

(He gathers a tape measure and other requisites of his profession, and hurries out.)

Mrs. Sowerberry. The sooner our jobs are done the better, too. Dishes, Charlotte, and beds!

(The women leave **Young Oliver** *and* **Noah Claypole** *alone on the stage.)*

Noah Claypole. D'you know what you are, Work'us? You're a sneak. That's what you are, a work'us sneak. Promotin' yer to mute, indeed, before yer've bin in the gime five minutes. I'll pull yer 'air, I will, if yer gives me 'arf a chance.

Oliver. In the course of the next few weeks, I acquired a great deal of experience, both of funerals and of Noah Claypole's malevolence and jealousy.

Noah Claypole. You'll be strung up one day, and I shan't 'arf 'ave a lot of fun watching yer struggle.

Oliver. Until the day arrived when I could stand Noah's taunts no longer. The crisis came when he attempted to be more facetious still, and in this attempt did what many small wits, with far greater reputations than Noah, sometimes do to this day when they want to be funny. He got rather personal.

Noah Claypole. Work'us! 'Ow's your mother?

Young Oliver. She's dead! Don't you say anything about her to me!

Noah Claypole. What did she die of, Work'us?

Young Oliver. Of a broken heart, some of our old nurses told me. I think I know what it must be to die of that!

Noah Claypole. Tol de rol de lairy, Work'us, what's set you a snivelling now?

Young Oliver. Not you. Don't think it.

Noah Claypole. Oh, not me, eh?

15

Young Oliver. No, not you. There; that's enough. Don't say anything more to me about her; you'd better not!

Noah Claypole. Better not! Well! Better not! Work'us, don't be impudent. Your mother, too! She was a nice one, she was. Oh, Lor! Yer know, Work'us, it can't be 'elped now, and I'm sure we must all pity yer very much, but yer must know—yer mother was a regular right-down bad 'un.

Young Oliver. What did you say?

Noah Claypole. A regular right-down bad 'un, Work'us. And it's a great deal better, Work'us, that she died when she did, or else she'd have been hard labouring in Bridewell, or transported, or 'ung; which is more likely than either, isn't it? . . .

(Crimson with fury, **Young Oliver** *seizes Noah Claypole by the throat; shakes him until his teeth chatter; and throws him to the ground.)*

. . . He'll murder me! Charlotte! Missis! Here's the new boy a-murdering of me! Help! Help! Oliver's gone mad! Char—lotte!

(Noah Claypole's shouts are responded to by a loud scream from **Charlotte***, and a louder one from* **Mrs. Sowerberry***.)*

Charlotte *(Rushing in and seizing Young Oliver).* Oh, you little wretch! Oh, you little un—grate—ful, mur—der—rous, hor—rid villain!

Mrs. Sowerberry *(Rushing in as soon as it is safe to do so).* Villain! Wretch! Murderer!

*(*Charlotte*,* **Mrs. Sowerberry** *and* **Noah Claypole** *scratch and pummel Young Oliver until they are all wearied out and can tear and beat no longer. Then they drag him, struggling and shouting, but nothing daunted, into the dust cellar and there lock him up.)*

Mrs. Sowerberry *(Sinking into a chair and bursting into tears).* Oh! Oooh! Ooooh!

Charlotte. Bless her, she's going off! A glass of water, Noah dear. Make haste!

Mrs. Sowerberry. Oh! Charlotte, what a mercy we have not all been murdered in our beds!

Charlotte. Ah! Mercy indeed, ma'am. I only hope this'll teach master not to have any more of these dreadful creatures, that are born to be murderers and robbers from their very cradle. Poor Noah! He was all but killed, ma'am, when I come in.

Mrs. Sowerberry. What's to be done? Your master's not at home; there's not a man in the house, and he'll kick that door down in ten minutes.

Charlotte. Dear, dear! I don't know, ma'am . . . unless we send for the police-officers.

Noah Claypole. Or the millingtary.

Mrs. Sowerberry. No! No! Run to Mr. Bumble, Noah, and tell him to come here directly, and not to lose a minute; never mind your cap! Make haste!

(Noah Claypole runs out, and pauses not once for breath until he reaches the Workhouse gate.)

Oliver. By the time Noah arrived back with Mr. Bumble, the position of affairs had not at all improved. Mr. Sowerberry had not yet returned, and I was continuing to kick with undiminished vigour at the cellar door . . .

(Mr. Bumble walks in, followed by Noah Claypole. Mrs. Sowerberry and Charlotte rush to the Beadle, and gesticulate wildly.)

. . . The accounts of my ferocity, as related by Mrs. Sowerberry and Charlotte, were of so startling a nature that Mr. Bumble judged it prudent to parley before opening the door.

Mr. Bumble *(Applying his mouth to the keyhole).* Oliver!

Young Oliver *(From inside).* Come; you let me out!

Mr. Bumble. Do you know this here voice, Oliver?

Young Oliver. Yes.

Mr. Bumble. Ain't you afraid of it, Sir? Ain't you a-trembling while I speak, Sir?

Young Oliver *(Boldly).* No!

(Mr. Bumble steps back from the keyhole, draws himself up to his full height, and looks from one to another of the by-standers in mute astonishment.)

Mrs. Sowerberry. Mr. Bumble, he must be mad! No boy in half his senses could venture to speak so to you.

Mr. Bumble. It's not Madness, ma'am. It's Meat.

Mrs. Sowerberry. What?

Mr. Bumble. Meat, ma'am, meat. You've over-fed him, ma'am. You've raised an artificial soul and spirit in him, ma'am, unbecoming a person of his condition: as the Board, Mrs. Sowerberry, who are practical philosophers, will tell you. What have paupers to do with soul or spirit? It's quite enough that we let 'em have live bodies. If you had kept the boy on gruel, ma'am, this would never have happened.

Mrs. Sowerberry. Dear, dear! This comes of being liberal!

Mr. Bumble. Ah! The only thing that can be done now, that I know of, is to leave him in the cellar for a day or so, till he's a little starved down; and then to take him out and keep him on gruel all through his apprenticeship. He comes of a bad family. Excitable natures, Mrs. Sowerberry! Both the nurse and doctor said that that mother of his made her way here against difficulties and pain that would have killed any well-disposed woman, weeks before.

*(***Young Oliver***, hearing enough to know that some new allusion is being made to his mother, recommences kicking with a violence that makes every other sound inaudible.* **Mr. Sowerberry** *returns at this juncture.)*

Mrs. Sowerberry. He tried to murder poor Noah. We had to send for Bumble.

*(***Mr. Sowerberry*** *unlocks the cellar door and drags out Young Oliver by the collar.)*

Mr. Sowerberry. Now, you are a nice young fellow, ain't you?

(He gives Young Oliver a shake and a box on the ear.)

Young Oliver. He called my mother names.

Mrs. Sowerberry. Well, and what if he did, you little ungrateful wretch? She deserved what he said, and worse.

Young Oliver. She didn't.

Mrs. Sowerberry. She did.

Young Oliver. It's a lie!

(That sends **Mrs. Sowerberry** *into hysterics. Her flood of tears leaves* **Mr. Sowerberry** *no alternative, and he gives Young Oliver a sound drubbing, which satisfies even Mrs. Sowerberry, and renders* **Mr. Bumble's** *subsequent application of the parochial cane rather unnecessary.)*

Oliver. I bore the lash without a cry: for I felt that pride swelling in my heart which would have kept down a shriek to the last, though they had roasted me alive . . .

(Mr. and Mrs. Sowerberry, Mr. Bumble, Charlotte and Noah Claypole leave Young Oliver alone as the light fades. He falls on his knees on the floor.)

. . . But when there were none to see or hear me, I wept such tears as God send, few so young may ever have had cause to pour out before me.

The candle was burning low in the socket when I rose to my feet. Having gazed cautiously around me, and listened intently, I gently undid the fastenings of the door and looked abroad. It was a cold, dark, sombre night, and I decided to leave that place for ever.

SCENE THREE
BARNET

*(The sun is rising in all its splendour, but the light only serves to remind Young Oliver of his own loneliness as he sinks down, with bleeding feet, and covered with dust, upon a door-step. A snub-nosed, flat-browed, common-faced boy, whom we shall know eventually as **Mr. Jack Dawkins** (alias **the Artful Dodger**) passes him carelessly and then returns and surveys him most earnestly from the opposite side of the street.)*

The Artful Dodger. Hullo, my covey! What's the row?

*(**Young Oliver** starts.)*

The Artful Dodger. Hullo, my covey! What's the row?

Young Oliver. I am very hungry and tired. I have walked a long way. I have been walking these seven days.

The Artful Dodger. Walking for sivin days! Oh, I see. You bin on the mill!

Young Oliver. What mill?

The Artful Dodger. What mill! Why, the tread mill, eh! Beak's orders, you know.

Young Oliver. Beak?

The Artful Dodger. My eyes, how green can a man be? Why, a beak's a madgistrate. Where was you dragged up? All right! All right! Don't tell me yit! Eh! You 'ungry or sumpfin? You want grub? . . .

(Young Oliver is almost too weak to nod.)

. . . Right, you shall 'ave it. I'm at low water mark myself—only got a bob and a tanner, but I'll fork out, if ye're skint. Stay there . . .

(Young Oliver tries to rise to his feet, but he has not succeeded before The Artful Dodger returns with a large ham roll. He gives this to Young Oliver, then he goes away again to fetch a half pint of beer.)

. . . Going to London?

Young Oliver. Yes.

The Artful Dodger. Got any lodgings?

Young Oliver. No.

The Artful Dodger. Money?

Young Oliver. No . . .

(The Artful Dodger whistles, and puts his arms into his pockets as far as his big coat sleeves will let them go.)

. . . Do you live in London?

The Artful Dodger. Yus. I does when I'm at home. I suppose you want some place to sleep in tonight, doncher?

Young Oliver. I do, indeed. I have not slept under a roof since I left the country.

The Artful Dodger. Don't fret your eyelids on that score. I've got to be in London tonight; and I know a 'spectable old genelman as lives there, wot'll give you lodgings for nothink, and never ask for the change—that is, if any genelman he knows interduces you. And don't 'e know me? Oh, no! Not in the least! By no means. Certainly not. 'E'll give you a comfortable place to stay, as sure as my name is Jack Dawkins. C'm on. We'll 'ave to look slippy if we're to get to Islington before the ale 'ouses shut.

SCENE FOUR
AT FAGIN'S

(A back room. The walls and ceiling of the room are black with age—it would be difficult to imagine a dirtier or more wretched place. Only a number of bright new or freshly washed silk hand-kerchiefs hanging over a clothes-horse relieve the monotony.

There is a shrill whistle from outside, followed by a knock. A very old shrivelled Jew comes in, his villainous-looking and repulsive face obscured by a quantity of matted red hair. He seems to be about to find out who whistled and knocked, then he hesitates, and goes back to the door through which he entered the room.)

Fagin *(Calling softly).* Bates! Charley Bates! Come here, my dear, will you? . . .

(A young gentleman as rough as the Artful Dodger swaggers in, and he is followed by three or four more boys who are no older than he. All are smoking long clay pipes and drinking spirits with the air of middle-aged men.)

. . . There's some one at the door, Charley. See who it is, will you, my sweet?

*(**Fagin** fades into the background as **Charley Bates** goes to answer the door.)*

Charley Bates *(calling out to the intruder).* Now then.

A Voice from below *(Giving the watchword).* Plummy and slam!

Charley Bates *(Peering outwards and shading his eyes with his hand).* There's two on you. Who's t'other one?

The Artful Dodger *(Pulling **Young Oliver** forward).* A new pal.

Charley Bates. Where did he come from?

The Artful Dodger. Greenland. Is Fagin in there?

Charley Bates. Yes, he's a-sortin' the wipes. Come in!

*(**The Artful Dodger** accepts the invitation. Then he sees Fagin and goes to whisper a few words in his ear. Then he turns round and grins at Young Oliver. So, too, does **Fagin**.)*

The Artful Dodger. This is him, Fagin. My friend Oliver Twist.

Fagin *(Making a low obeisance to Young Oliver, and taking him by the*

21

hand). My dear, I hope that I will have the honour of your intimate acquaintance . . .

(The young gentlemen with the pipes crowd round Young Oliver and shake his hands very hard—especially the one in which he still holds his little bundle. One young gentleman takes his hat and another saves him the trouble of emptying his own pockets. These civilities would probably be extended further, but for **Fagin's** *liberal exercise of a toasting fork on the heads and shoulders of the affectionate youths who are offering them.)*

. . . We are very glad to see you, Oliver, very. Dodger, go and take off the sausages . . . Ah, you're a-staring at the pocket-handkerchiefs! Eh, my dear! There are a good many of 'em, ain't there? We've just looked them out ready for the wash; that's all, Oliver; that's all! Ha! Ha! Ha! And now, my dears, you must git to your beds if you're going to see the fun at Newgate in the morning.

(The light fades, and Fagin's 'young gentlemen' go out.)

Oliver. I slept, that night, on the floor, on a rough bed made of old sacks . . .

(When the stage becomes light again, **Young Oliver** *is lying in one corner of the room, and* **Fagin** *is stirring some coffee in a saucepan and whistling softly to himself.)*

Oliver. It was late next morning when I awoke from a sound long sleep into that drowsy state between sleeping and waking in which one is half conscious of everything that is passing around, without being personally engaged.

Fagin *(To see if Young Oliver is awake).* Oliver! Oliver Twist! My dear! . . .

*(***Young Oliver** *does not stir, so* **Fagin** *produces a small box from some hiding place. He opens the box and takes from it a magnificent gold watch.)*

. . . Aha! Clever dogs! Clever dogs! Staunch to the last! Never told the old parson where they were. Never peached upon old Fagin! And why should they? It wouldn't have loosened the knot, or kept the drop up, a minute longer. No, no, no! Fine fellows! Fine fellows! . . .

(He pulls more jewellery from the box.)

. . . What a fine thing capital punishment is! Dead men never repent; dead men never bring awkward stories to light. Ah, it's a fine thing for the trade! Five of 'em strung up in a row, and none left to play booty, or turn white-livered! . . .

(His bright dark eyes, which have been staring vacantly before him, fall on Young Oliver's face. Instantly, he closes the lid of the box with a loud crash, and, laying his hand on a bread knife, starts furiously up.)

. . . What's that? What do you watch me for? Why are you awake? What have you seen? Speak out, boy! Quick—quick! For your life!

Young Oliver *(Meekly).* I wasn't able to sleep any longer, sir. I am very sorry if I have disturbed you, sir.

Fagin. You were not awake an hour ago?

Young Oliver. No! No, indeed!

Fagin *(With a threatening attitude).* Are you sure?

Young Oliver. Upon my word I was not, Sir. I was not, indeed, sir.

Fagin. Tush, tush, my dear! Of course I know that, my dear. I only tried to frighten you. You're a brave boy. Ha! ha! You're a brave boy, Oliver! . . .

*(**Fagin** rubs his hands with a chuckle, but he glances uneasily at the box, notwithstanding.)*

. . . Did you see any of these pretty things, my dear?

(He lays his hand on the box.)

Young Oliver. Yes, sir.

Fagin. Ah! . . .

(He turns rather pale.)

. . . They're—they're mine, Oliver; my little property. All I have to live upon, in my old age. The folks call me a miser, my dear. Only a miser, that's all . . . Now, there's a pitcher of water in that corner by the door. Bring it here; and I'll give you a basin to wash in, my dear . . .

*(**Young Oliver** walks across the room and stoops for an instant to

23

raise the pitcher. When he turns, the box has gone.)

. . . Empty the basin out of the window, my dear, when you've finished . . .

(There is a shrill whistle outside. **Fagin** *hears the pass-words 'plummy and slam!', then he admits* **the Artful Dodger** *and* **Charley Bates,** *who have been out on a foray.)*

. . . Well! . . .

(He addresses himself to the Artful Dodger)

. . . I hope you've been at work this morning, my dears?

The Artful Dodger. 'Ard.

Charley Bates. As nails.

Fagin. Good boys, good boys! What have you got, Dodger?

The Artful Dodger. A couple of pocket-books.

Fagin. Lined?

The Artful Dodger. Pretty well.

(He produces two pocket-books.)

Fagin *(After looking at the insides carefully).* Not so heavy as they might be, but very neat and nicely made. Ingenious workman, ain't he, Oliver?

Young Oliver. Very, indeed, sir.

*(***Charley Bates*** laughs uproariously- very much to the amazement of* **Young Oliver,** *who sees nothing to laugh at in anything that has passed.)*

Fagin *(To Charley Bates).* And what have you got, my dear?

Charley Bates *(Producing four pocket-handkerchiefs).* Wipes.

Fagin *(Inspecting them closely).* Well, they're very good ones, very. You haven't marked them well, though, Charley; so the marks shall be picked out with a needle, and we'll teach Oliver how to do it. Shall us, Oliver, eh? Ha! Ha! Ha!

Young Oliver. If you please, sir.

Fagin. You'd like to be able to make pocket-handkerchiefs as easy as Charley Bates, wouldn't you, my dear?

Young Oliver. Very much, indeed, if you'll teach me, sir.

*(***Charley Bates*** sees something so exquisitely ludicrous in this*

reply that he laughs until he is in danger of suffocation.)

Charley Bates. Oh . . . oh . . . oh . . . He is so jolly green!

The Artful Dodger *(Smoothing Young Oliver's hair over his eyes).* He'll know better, by-and-bye.

Fagin. You watch our little game, Oliver. It's a jolly game, isn't it, boys? I'll put my snuff-box in here . . .

(He puts it in one pocket of his trousers.)

. . . a notecase in here . . .

(He puts it in the other pocket.)

. . . a watch in here . . .

(He puts it in his waistcoat pocket.)

. . . and a diamond pin in here . . .

(He sticks a mock diamond pin in his shirt.)

. . . Now, I'm a respectable old gentleman, out for a walk in the streets . . .

(He trots up and down the room with a stick.)

. . . You watch me . . .

(Sometimes he stops at the fireplace and sometimes at the door, making believe that he is staring with all his might into shop windows. **The Artful Dodger** *and* **Charley Bates** *follow him closely, getting out of his sight, so nimbly, every time he turns round, that it is impossible to follow their motions. At last,* **the Artful Dodger** *treads upon his toes and* **Charley Bates** *stumbles up against him behind, so that in one moment they take from him with the most extraordinary rapidity his snuff box, notecase, shirt pin and pocket handkerchief. Then* **Fagin** *feels a hand in one of his pockets.)*

. . . Got you! Ain't I got you! Aha! Aha! Aha! There's a hand in my hip pocket there! I'll teach you! I'll teach you! I'll teach you!

*(***Fagin** *picks up his toasting fork and starts to chase* **the Artful Dodger** *and* **Charley Bates** *round the room. While he is doing this,* **Bill Sikes** *enters. Sikes, who is a stoutly built ruffian, is followed by* **Nancy,** *his girl.)*

25

Bill Sikes. What are you up to, eh? Ill-treating the boys, you covetous, avaricious, in-sa-ti-a-ble old fence? I wonder they don't murder you! I would if I was them. If I'd been your 'prentice, I'd have done it long ago, and—no, I couldn't have sold you afterwards, for you're fit for nothing but keeping as a curiosity of ugliness in a glass bottle, and I suppose they don't blow glass bottles large enough.

Fagin. Hush! Hush! Mr. Sikes! Don't speak so loud!

Bill Sikes. None of your mistering. You always mean mischief when you come that. You know my name: out with it! I shan't disgrace it when the time comes.

Fagin. Well, well, then—Bill Sikes. You seem out of humour, Bill.

Bill Sikes. Perhaps I am. I should think you was rather out of sorts, too, unless you means no 'arm by yer blabbing, and yer . . .

Fagin. Are you mad?

(He catches Bill Sikes by the sleeve and points towards the boys. **Mr. Sikes** *contents himself with tying an imaginary knot under his left ear, and jerking his head over on the right shoulder: a piece of dumb show which the Jew appears to understand perfectly.)*

. . . Here, boys . . .

*(***Fagin** *produces a few shillings from some secret hiding place and gives them to the Artful Dodger.)*

. . . Go out and buy us some sausages—er, *beef* sausages, my dear—and anything else you fancy while I give Bill Sikes a glass of liquor.

(The boys take Fagin's money and go.)

Bill Sikes. And mind you don't poison it.

*(***Fagin** *gets out liquor, and glasses, and gives a glass of spirits to Bill Sikes, and one to Nancy.)*

Fagin. What do you want, Bill?

Bill Sikes. Blunt, you withered old fence, that's what I want—blunt. What the hell else do you think I would want?

Fagin. Well, what have you brought me, my dear? . . .

*(***Bill Sikes** *produces, from a capacious inside pocket, a pair of*

silver candlesticks and a pair of silver salad servers. **Fagin** *inspects them closely.)*

. . . Those aren't bad at all, Bill, they aren't bad at all.

Bill Sikes. Five pounds, I wants for 'em.

Fagin *(With a gesture of despair).* Bill Sikes, you'll be the ruin of me! Two pounds, and not one penny more.

Bill Sikes. Give us 'em back, then. I'll take 'em where they're wanted.

Fagin. Three, Bill . . .

*(***Bill Sikes** *shakes his head.)*

. . . Three pounds three?

*(***Bill Sikes** *shakes his head again.)*

. . . Three guineas?

(Another shake.)

. . . Allright, then, Bill, I'll meet you. Three pounds four shillings and sixpence. That's the right price, my dear. That's all I'll get in the market.

Bill Sikes. Well, if you won't give me any more, I suppose I must be content with that. Come on. Hand over.

Fagin. I'll settle up when I see you next, Bill. I've just given the boys money for sausages. I've only got eighteen-pence left to keep house with.

Bill Sikes. Come on, you old skinflint. You've got plenty more locked away.

Fagin. I've got none to lock up, my dear—Ha!Ha!Ha!—None to lock up. It's a poor trade, this one is, and no thanks; but I'm fond of seeing the young people about me; and I bear it all, I bear it all.

Bill Sikes. That's all very well, Fagin, but I must have some blunt from you before tonight.

Fagin. I haven't a piece of coin about me.

Bill Sikes. Then you've got lots at the other ken. I must have some from there.

Fagin. Lots! . . .

(He holds up his hands.)

. . . I haven't so much as would . . .

Bill Sikes. I don't know how much you've got, and I dare say you

27

hardly know yourself, it'd take that long to count, but I must have some tonight, and that's flat.

Fagin. Well, well. I'll send the Artful round, presently.

Bill Sikes. You won't do nothing of the kind . . .

(The Artful Dodger and Charley Bates creep back into the room.)

. . . That Dodger's a deal too artful. 'E'd forgit to come, or lose his way, or get dodged by traps and so be prewented, or anything for an excuse, if you put him up to it. No, Nancy shall go to the ken and fetch it, to make all sure—she'll be round while I'm 'aving my kip. Don't you fergit she's coming, will yer? Or else . . . C'mon.

(With a jerk of his head he signals to Nancy, who follows him out.)

The Artful Dodger. Sausages, Fagin! . . .

(He throws them across.)

. . . Beef sausages!

Fagin. Good boy! Good boy! Here! Here's two shillings! Now, you and Charley go and enjoy yourselves! . . .

(The Artful Dodger and Charley Bates take the money and make off.)

. . . There, my dear . . .

(Fagin speaks to Young Oliver.)

. . . That's a pleasant life, isn't it? They have gone out for the day.

Young Oliver. Have they finished work, Sir?

Fagin. Yes, that is, unless they should unexpectedly come across any when they are out: and they won't neglect it if they do, my dear, depend upon it. Make 'em your models, my dear. Do everything they bid you, and take their advice in all matters— especially the Dodger's, my dear. He'll be a great man himself, and will make you one too if you take pattern by him.—Is my handkerchief hanging out of my pocket, my dear?

Young Oliver. Yes, Sir.

Fagin. See if you can take it out without my feeling it: as you saw them do when we were at play, just now . . .

(Young Oliver holds up the bottom of the pocket with one hand,

as he has seen the Dodger do, and he draws the handkerchief lightly out of it with the other.)

. . . Is it gone?

Young Oliver. Here it is, Sir.

Fagin *(Patting Young Oliver on the head approvingly).* You're a clever boy, my dear. I never saw a sharper lad. Here's a shilling for you. If you go on in this way you'll be the greatest man of the time. And now come in here, and I'll show you how to take the marks out of the handkerchieves.

(He leads Young Oliver to the inner recesses of his den.)

Oliver. At the end of a month, I was reasonably proficient at the pocket-handkerchief game. By that time, I was beginning to languish, for want of fresh air, and I earnestly entreated the old gentleman, on many occasions, that he should allow me to go out to work with my two companions.

At length, one morning, I obtained the permission I had so eagerly sought. There had been no handkerchieves to work on for two or three days and the dinners at Fagin's had become, in consequence, decidedly meagre.

*(***Fagin** *comes in, with* **Young Oliver.** **The Artful Dodger** *follows, with* **Charley Bates***.)*

Fagin. Oliver, here's a cap for you. I'm letting you go out this morning.

Young Oliver. Out?

Fagin. Out. With the Dodger and Charley . . .

(He turns to the other boys)

. . . I am letting you take young Oliver with you today, Dodger, and I want you and Charley Bates to keep a sharp eye on him. Bring him back safely, my dearest, or I'll C...H...U...C...K you down the S...T...A...I...R...S.

The Artful Dodger. Right you are, Fagin. Trust your old Dodger.

Fagin. He's green, but he's . . .

*(***Fagin** *stops, as he sees the dark, cloaked figure of* **Monks** *appear on the threshold.)*

. . . Mr. Monks, sir.

Monks. A word with you, Mr. Fagin, please.

Fagin. Certainly, Mr. Monks. I'll send the boys off, then we'll have some peace and quiet.

(He makes a sign.)

The Artful Dodger. Come on, Oliver. Time to pad the hoof.

(The boys go out. **Monks** *starts, when he sees Young Oliver.)*

Monks. That boy, Mr. Fagin! Who is that boy?

Fagin. He's just a lad the Dodger found, Mr. Monks. He has a very interesting history.

Monks. His face seems oddly familiar to me, Mr. Fagin. I think, perhaps, I might be very interested to hear that history. Will you share it with me?

Fagin. For the right consideration, Mr. Monks. Will you please to step this way?

(He leads Monks off to his sanctum.)

Oliver. In spite of Fagin's admonitions the Artful Dodger and Charley Bates did not bring me back safely. They returned to Fagin's without me, very shortly after he had successfully got rid of his visitor Monks.

*(***Fagin*** *enters, with a pewter pot in one hand and the toasting fork in the other. There is a sausage on the end of the fork.)*

Fagin. There's money in this for me . . . Big, big, money for me . . .

(There are footsteps on the stairs. He bends his ear towards the door and listens.)

. . . Here they are . . .

(His countenance changes.)

. . . Why, how's this? Only two of 'em? Where's the third? They can't have got into trouble. Hark! . . .

(The footsteps reach the landing. The door is slowly opened; and **the Artful Dodger** *and* **Charley Bates** *come in.)*

. . . Where's Oliver? Where's the boy? . . .

(The young thieves make no reply.)

. . . What's become of the boy? . . .

(Fagin seizes the Artful Dodger tightly by the collar.)

. . . Speak out, or I'll throttle you . . .

(He shakes the Dodger.)

. . . Will you speak?

The Artful Dodger *(Sullenly)*. Why, the traps have got him, and that's all about it.

Fagin. The traps have got him.

The Artful Dodger. We was on a prime plant, an old gent lookin' in at a bookstall, and just as we was right on 'is fogle, that Oliver must 'ave seen what we was up to and 'e started to 'op it. You should ha' 'eard the row they set up! 'Stop thief! Stop thief! Stop thief!, Yer never 'eard such a din. Like a pack of ahnds, they was. Well, 'e give 'em a good run, but they nabbed 'im at last, down by Clerkenwell Green, and Charley 'ere and I got clear away while they took 'im off to the Beak's Office. And now, let go o' me, will yer?

(With one jerk, the **Artful Dodger** *swings himself out of his big coat, which he leaves in Fagin's hands. Then he snatches the toasting fork and makes a pass at Fagin with it.* **Fagin** *seizes the pot of beer and hurls the contents at the Dodger. The beer hits* **Bill Sikes,** *who has just come through the door, followed by* **Nancy.***)*

Bill Sikes. Why, what the blazes is this? Who pitched that 'ere at me? I might 'ave knowed as nobody but a rich, plundering old fence could afford to throw good drink away. Wot's it all about, Fagin?

Fagin. The boy . . . Young Oliver . . . The traps have got him . . . He was out with the Dodger.

The Artful Dodger. It were a prime plant, too.

Bill Sikes. Well, what's ter that, eh? 'E won't git scragged.

Fagin. I'm afraid that he may say something which will get us into trouble.

Bill Sikes *(With a malicious grin)*. That's very likely. You're blowed upon, Fagin.

Fagin. And I'm afraid, you see, if the game was up with us, it might be up with a good many more, and that it would come out rather worse for you than it would for me, my dear.

Bill Sikes. Somebody must find out wot's been done at the Beak's office . . .

(Fagin nods.)

. . . If he hasn't peached, and is committed, there's no fear till he comes out again, and then he must be taken care on. You must get hold of him somehow.

Fagin *(Nodding again).* You'll go, then, Mr. Sikes?

Bill Sikes. Me? No. I ain't goin' near any Police office not fer anythink. Whaddya think I am?

Fagin. Dodger?

The Artful Dodger. Not on your nelly. Cahnt me aht.

Charley Bates. Nor me neither, Fagin.

Fagin. Nancy will go; won't you, my dear?

Nancy. Wheres?

Fagin. Only just up to the office, my dear.

Nancy. I'll be blessed if I will, Fagin, so it's no use a-trying that on.

Bill Sikes. What do you mean by that?

Nancy. What I say, Bill.

Bill Sikes. Why, you're just the very person to go. Nobody about here knows anything of you.

Nancy. And as I don't want 'em to, neither, it's rather more 'no' than 'yes' with me, Bill.

Bill Sikes. She'll go, Fagin.

Nancy. No, she won't, Fagin.

Bill Sikes. Yes, she will, Fagin. Won't yer, Nancy? . . .

(He goes close to her and gives her a look that is full of significance.)

. . . Won't yer, Nancy?

Nancy *(Submissively).* Yes, Bill.

Bill Sikes. There's me dear.

Fagin. Put this white apron on, Nancy . . .

(He ties an apron over her gown.)

. . . And this bonnet . . .

32

(He finds one from his inexhaustible stock.)

. . . Carry this in one hand . . .

(He gives her a little covered basket.)

. . . It looks more respectable, dear.

Bill Sikes. Give her a door-key to carry in her t'other one, Fagin. It looks real and genivine like.

Fagin. Yes, yes, my dear, so it does . . .

(He hangs a street-door key on her forefinger.)

. . . There, very good! Very good indeed, my dear!

Nancy *(Feigning distress).* Oh, my brother! My poor, dear, sweet, innocent little brother! What has become of him? Where have they taken him to? Oh, do have pity and tell me what's been done with the dear boy, gentlemen; do, gentlemen, if you please, gentlemen!

(She pauses, winks to the company, nods smilingly round, and disappears.)

Fagin. Ah! She's a clever girl, my dears!

Bill Sikes *(As they follow her out).* She's an honour to her sex. Here's her health, and wishing they was all like her!

SCENE FIVE
AT MR. BROWNLOW'S

Oliver. But I had not been sent to prison. Struck by my strange resemblance to a picture in his house—the likeness of a poor girl who had been dead for many years—the old gentleman refused to bring a charge against me, or to offer any evidence. Instead, he took me to his home. There I was bathed, and fed, and nursed through a fever that assailed me as a result of my privations.

They were happy days, those of my recovery. Everybody was kind and gentle, and after the noise and turbulence in the midst of which I had always lived, it seemed like Heaven itself.

As soon as I was strong enough to put on a new suit of clothes, Mr. Brownlow, my benefactor, sent for me.

(Mr. Brownlow is in his comfortable study. He tugs a bell-pull, which brings Mrs. Bedwin, his housekeeper, to him.)

Mr. Brownlow. Ah, Mrs. Bedwin, and how is young Oliver this evening?

Mrs. Bedwin. Very happy, Sir, if I may say so, and very grateful indeed for your goodness.

Mr. Brownlow. When he has finished his dinner, will you be good enough to ask him to step down here for a few minutes?

Mrs. Bedwin. He's finished now, Sir. I'll go and tell him you want him.

(She goes to fetch Young Oliver. In a moment the boy knocks quietly on the door.)

Mr. Brownlow. Ah, Oliver! Come in a moment! Come in, and sit down! . . .

(Young Oliver complies, and surveys with curiosity the shelves that reach from the floor to the ceiling.)

. . . There are a good many books, are there not, my boy?

Young Oliver. A great number, Sir. I never saw so many.

Mr. Brownlow. You shall read them, if you behave well, and you will like that better than looking at the outsides—that is, in some cases; because there are books of which the backs and covers are by far the best parts . . .

(Young Oliver smiles.)

. . . How should you like to grow up a clever man, and write books, eh?

Young Oliver. I think I would rather read them, Sir.

Mr. Brownlow. What! Wouldn't you like to be a bookwriter?

Young Oliver *(After a little consideration).* I should think it would be a much better thing to be a book-seller, Sir.

Mr. Brownlow *(To himself, having laughed at Young Oliver's earnest answer).* Curious instinct the young have for self-preservation . . .

(He speaks to Young Oliver.)

. . . Now, I want you to pay great attention, my boy, to what I am going to say. I shall talk to you without any reserve, because I am sure you are as well able to understand me as many older persons would be.

34

Young Oliver *(Alarmed at Mr. Brownlow's serious tone)*. Oh, don't tell me you are going to send me away, Sir, pray! Don't turn me out of doors to wander in the streets again. Let me stay here and be your servant. Don't send me back to the wretched place I came from. Have mercy upon a poor boy, Sir!

Mr. Brownlow. My dear child, you need not be afraid of my deserting you, unless you give me cause.

Young Oliver. I never, never will, Sir.

Mr. Brownlow. I hope not. I do not think you ever will. I have been deceived, before, in the objects whom I have endeavoured to benefit; but I feel strongly disposed to trust you, nevertheless. You say you are an orphan, without a friend in the world; all the inquiries I have been able to make confirm the statement. Let me hear the rest of your story; where you came from; who brought you up; and how you got into the company in which I found you. Speak the truth, and you shall not be friendless while I live.

*(***Young Oliver** *is about to start, when there is an impatient knock on the street-door.* **Mrs. Bedwin** *comes to announce a visitor.)*

Mrs. Bedwin. It's Mr. Grimwig, Sir.

Mr. Brownlow. Is he coming up?

Mrs. Bedwin. Yes, Sir. He asked if there were any muffins in the house; and when I told him yes, he said he had come to tea.

Mr. Brownlow *(To Young Oliver)*. This is a very old friend of mine, Oliver. You must not mind him being a little rough in his manners. He's worthy enough at heart.

Young Oliver. Shall I go downstairs, Sir?

Mr. Brownlow. No. I would rather you remained here.

*(***Mr. Grimwig** *walks into the room.)*

Mr. Grimwig. Look here! Do you see this! Isn't it a most wonderful and extraordinary thing that I can't call at a man's house but I find a piece of orange peel on the staircase. Orange peel! Orange peel will be my death, or I'll be content to eat my own . . . Hello! . . . .

(He notices Young Oliver, and retreats a pace or two.)

. . . What's that?

Mr. Brownlow. This is young Oliver Twist, whom we were speaking about.

(Young Oliver bows.)

Mr. Grimwig. If that's not the boy, Sir, who had the orange, and threw this bit of peel upon the staircase, I'll eat my head, and his too.

Mr. Brownlow *(Laughing).* No, no, he has not had one. Come! Put down your hat; and speak to my young friend.

Mr. Grimwig. How are you, boy?

Young Oliver. A great deal better, thank you, Sir.

Mr. Brownlow. Step downstairs and tell Mrs. Bedwin we are ready for tea, will you, Oliver?

Young Oliver. Certainly, Sir.

(He goes out.)

Mr. Brownlow. He is a nice-looking boy, is he not?

Mr. Grimwig *(Pettishly).* I don't know.

Mr. Brownlow. Don't know?

Mr. Grimwig. No. I don't know. I never see any difference in boys. I only know two sorts of boys. Mealy boys, and beef-faced boys.

Mr. Brownlow. And which is Oliver?

Mr. Grimwig. Mealy. I know a friend who has a beef-faced boy; a fine boy, they call him; with a round head, and red cheeks, and glaring eyes; a horrid boy; with a body and limbs that appear to be swelling out of the seams of his blue clothes; with the voice of a pilot, and the appetite of a wolf. I know him! The wretch!

Mr. Brownlow. Come, these are not the characteristics of young Oliver Twist; so he needn't excite your wrath.

Mr. Grimwig. He may have worse. He may have worse, I say. Where does he come from? Who is he? What is he? He has had a fever. What of that? Fevers are not peculiar to good people, are they? Bad people have fevers sometimes; haven't they, eh? I knew a man who was hung in Jamaica for murdering his master. He had had a fever six times; he wasn't recommended to mercy on that account. Pooh! Nonsense!

(Mrs. Bedwin comes in to lay a table for tea. She is followed by Young Oliver.)

Mrs. Bedwin. May we come in, Sir?

Mr. Brownlow. Certainly, Mrs. Bedwin.

(She starts to spread a table-cloth, helped by Young Oliver.)

Mr. Grimwig *(With a certain amount of malice).* And when are we going to hear a full, true and particular account of the life and adventure of Oliver Twist?

Mr. Brownlow. Oliver is in the middle of his account, my good friend, but I prefer that he shall be alone with me while he does so . . .

(He turns to Young Oliver.)

. . . Come up to me tomorrow morning at ten o'clock, my dear.

Young Oliver. Yes, Sir.

(There is a knock at the street-door. **Mrs. Bedwin** *goes to see who is there.* **Young Oliver** *follows her, so that he can help to carry in the tea-things.)*

Mr. Grimwig. I'll tell you what. He won't come up to you tomorrow morning. I saw him hesitate. He is deceiving you, my good friend.

Mr. Brownlow. I'll swear he is not. I'll answer for that boy's truth with my life!

Mr. Grimwig. And I for his falsehood with my head!

Mr. Brownlow. We shall see.

Mr. Grimwig *(With a provoking smile).* We will!

*(***Mrs. Bedwin** *returns, with a small parcel.)*

Mrs. Bedwin. It's the books you ordered, Sir.

Mr. Brownlow. Ah, stop the boy, Mrs. Bedwin. There is something to go back.

Mrs. Bedwin. He has gone, Sir.

Mr. Brownlow. Call after him, will you? It's particular. He is a poor man, and they are not paid for. There are some books to be taken back, too.

*(***Mrs. Bedwin** *hurries out. In a moment she is back, followed by* **Young Oliver.***)*

Mrs. Bedwin. I'm sorry, Sir. He was right out of sight.

Mr. Brownlow. Dear me, I am very sorry for that. I particularly wished those books to be returned tonight.

Mr. Grimwig. Send Oliver with them. He will be sure to deliver them safely, you know.

Young Oliver. Yes, do let me take them, Sir. I'll run all the way.

*(***Mr. Brownlow** *is just going to say that Young Oliver shall not*

go out on any account when a malicious cough from **Mr. Grimwig**
causes him to change his mind.)

Mr. Brownlow. You shall go, my dear. Those are the books, over there . .

*(***Young Oliver** *picks up the books that are to be returned.)*

. . . You are to say that you have brought those books back, and
that you have come to pay the four pound ten I owe him. This is
a five-pound note, so you will have to bring me back ten shillings
change.

Young Oliver. I won't be ten minutes, Sir.

(He buttons up the bank-note in his jacket pocket.)

Mrs. Bedwin. Here's your cap, my dear, and your muffler . . .

(She accompanies him to the door, fussing as she goes.)

. . . You mustn't catch cold. The evenings are very treacherous
at this time of year.

Mr. Brownlow. Let me see; he'll be back in twenty minutes, at the
longest . . .

(He pulls out his watch.)

. . . It will be dark, by that time.

Mr. Grimwig. Oh! You really expect him to come back, do you?

Mr. Brownlow. Don't you?

Mr. Grimwig. No! I do not. The boy has a new suit of clothes on his
back, a set of valuable books under his arm, and a five-pound
note in his pocket. He'll join his old friends the thieves and laugh
at you. If ever that boy returns to this house, Sir, I'll eat my
head.

Mr. Brownlow. Come up to the parlour, my friend. We'll watch for
him.

SCENE SIX
A STREET

*(***Young Oliver** *is walking along, thinking how happy and
contented he ought to feel, when* **Nancy** *appears and throws her
arms tightly round his neck.)*

38

Young Oliver. Don't! Let go of me! Who is it? What are you stopping me for?

Nancy. Oh my gracious! I've found him! Oh! Oliver! Oliver! Oh, you naughty boy, to make me suffer so! Come home, dear, come. Oh, I've found him. Thank gracious goodness heavins, I've found him! . . .

(A small crowd gathers, as **Nancy** *becomes hysterical.)*

. . . Come home directly, you cruel boy! Come!

First Bystander. What's the matter, ma'am?

Nancy. He ran away, near a month ago, from his parents, who are hardworking and respectable people; and went and joined a set of thieves and bad characters; and almost broke his mother's heart.

Second Bystander. Young wretch!

First Bystander. Go home, do, you little brute!

Young Oliver. I am not. I don't know her. I haven't any sister, or father or mother either. I'm an orphan; I live at Highbury.

Nancy. Only hear him, how he braves it out!

Young Oliver. Why, it's Nancy!

Nancy. You see, he knows me! He can't help himself. Make him come home, there's good people, or he'll kill his dear mother and father, and break my heart!

Bill Sikes *(Bursting out of a beer-shop).* What the devil's this? Young Oliver! Come home to your poor mother, you young dog! Come 'ome, will yer?

Young Oliver *(Struggling).* I don't belong to them. I don't know them! Help! Help!

Bill Sikes. Help! Yus, I'll 'elp you, yer young rascal! What books is these? You've been a-stealing 'em, 'ave yer? Give 'em 'ere.

*(***Bill Sikes** *tears the volumes from Young Oliver's grasp and bangs the boy with them.)*

First Bystander. That's right! That's the only way of bringing him to his senses!

Second Bystander. To be sure!

Third Bystander. It'll do him good!

Bill Sikes. He shall have it, too! Come on, you young villain!

(He picks up Young Oliver, and carries him off.)

39

Oliver. The gas-lamps were lighted; Mrs. Bedwin waited anxiously at the open door; the servant ran up the street twenty times to see if there were any sign of my return; and still the two old gentlemen sat, perseveringly, in the dark parlour, with the watch between them. They waited in vain.

ACT TWO

SCENE ONE
THE MATRON'S ROOM, AT THE WORKHOUSE

(Mrs. Corney is about to make herself a pot of tea. At the fireplace, the smallest of all possible kettles is singing in the smallest of all possible voices.)

Mrs. Corney. Well, I'm sure we have all on us a great deal to be grateful for! A great deal, if we did but know it. Ah! . . .

(The teapot, being very easily filled, runs over and the water slightly scalds Mrs. Corney's hand.)

. . . Drat the pot! A little stupid thing, that only holds a couple of cups! What use is it to anybody! Except to a poor desolate creature like me. Oh, dear! . . .

(In her mind, there are awakened sad recollections of Mr. Corney who has been dead for more than five-and-twenty years.)

. . . I shall never get another! I shall never get another—like him! . . .

(There is a soft tap at the room-door.)

. . . Oh, come in with you! Some of the old women dying, I suppose. They always die when I'm at meals. Don't stand there letting the cold air in, don't. What's amiss now, eh?

The voice of Mr. Bumble. Nothing, Ma'am, nothing.

Mrs. Corney *(Her voice suddenly sweet again).* Dear me! Is that Mr. Bumble?

Mr. Bumble. At your service, Madam.

(He now makes his appearance, bearing a cocked hat in one hand and a bundle in the other.)

Mrs. Corney. Hard weather, Mr. Bumble.

Mr. Bumble. Hard, indeed, ma'am. Anti-porochial weather this, ma'am. We have given away, Mrs. Corney, we have given away a

41

matter of twenty quartern loaves and a cheese and a half this
very blessed afternoon; and yet them paupers are not contented.

Mrs. Corney. Of course not. When would they be, Mr. Bumble?

Mr. Bumble. I never see anything like the pitch it's got to. The day
afore yesterday, a man—you have been a married woman, ma'am,
and I may mention it to you—a man, with hardly a rag upon his
back . . .

*(*Mrs. Corney *looks modestly at the floor.)*

. . . goes to our overseer's door when he has got company coming
to dinner; and says, he must be relieved, Mrs. Corney. As he
wouldn't go away, and shocked the company very much, our
overseer sent him out a pound of potatoes and half a pint of
oatmeal. 'My heart!' says the ungrateful villain, 'what's the use
of this to me? You might as well give me a pair of iron spectacles!'
'Very good,' says our overseer, taking 'em away again, 'you won't
get anything else here.' 'Then I'll die in the streets!' says the
vagrant. 'Oh no, you won't,' says our overseer.

Mrs. Corney. Ha! Ha! That was very good! So like Mr. Grannett,
wasn't it? Well, Mr. Bumble?

Mr. Bumble. Well, ma'am, he went away; and he did die in the streets.
There's an obstinate pauper for you!

Mrs. Corney. It beats anything I could have believed!

Mr. Bumble. But these are official secrets, ma'am; not to be spoken of,
except, as I may say, among the porochial officers such as
ourselves . . .

(He stops to unpack his bundle.)

. . . This is the port wine, ma'am, that the Board ordered for the
infirmary; real, fresh, genuine port wine; only out of the cask
this forenoon; clear as a bell; and no sediment!

*(He holds the bottles up to the light, and shakes them well to
test their excellence. Then he puts them down and takes up his
hat, as if to go.)*

Mrs. Corney. You'll have a very cold walk, Mr. Bumble.

Mr. Bumble *(Turning up his coat collar).* It blows, ma'am, enough to
cut one's ears off.

Mrs. Corney. Would you not care, Mr. Bumble, for a little cup of tea?

Mr. Bumble. Why, thank you, ma'am, I don't mind if I do.

(He turns back his collar and lays his hat and stick upon a chair. Then he draws another chair up to Mrs. Corney's table and sits down.)

Mrs. Corney *(Taking up the sugar-basin)*. Sweet? Mr. Bumble?

Mr. Bumble. Very sweet indeed, ma'am. . .

(He fixes his eyes on Mrs. Corney as he says this. She colours, as she passes him his tea.)

. . . You have a cat, ma'am, I see. And kittens too, I declare!

Mrs. Corney. I am so fond of them, Mr. Bumble, you can't think. They're so happy, so frolicsome and so cheerful that they are quite companions for me.

Mr. Bumble *(Approvingly)*. Very nice animals, ma'am. So very domestic.

Mrs. Corney *(With enthusiasm)*. Oh, yes! So fond of their home, too, that it's quite a pleasure, I'm sure.

Mr. Bumble. Mrs. Corney, ma'am, I mean to say this, ma'am; that any cat, or kitten, that could live with you, ma'am, and not be fond of its home, must be a ass, ma'am.

Mrs. Corney. Oh, Mr. Bumble!

Mrs. Bumble. It's of no use disguising facts, ma'am, . .

(He flourishes his teaspoon.)

. . . I would drown it myself, with pleasure.

Mrs. Corney *(Vivaciously)*. Then you're a cruel man . . .

(She holds out her hand for Mr. Bumble's cup.)

. . . and a very hard-hearted man besides.

Mr. Bumble. Hard-hearted, ma'am?

(He squeezes Mrs. Corney's little finger.)

. . . Hard?

(He moves his chair round the table, to diminish the distance between himself and Mrs. Corney.)

. . . Are you hard-hearted, Mrs. Corney?

Mrs. Corney. Dear me! What a very curious question from a single man. What can you want to know for, Mr. Bumble? . . .

(Mr. Bumble drinks his tea to the last drop, wipes his lips, and deliberately kisses the matron.)

. . . Mr. Bumble! Mr. Bumble, I shall scream! . . .

(In a slow and dignified manner Mr. Bumble puts his arm round the matron's waist. Before she can scream, there is a loud knocking at the door, and her preparations are rendered unnecessary.)

. . . Who's there?

(Mr. Bumble darts with great agility to the wine bottles and begins to dust them with great violence.)

A Female Pauper *(At the door).* If you please, mistress, Old Sally is a-going fast.

Mrs. Corney. Well, what's that to me? I can't keep her alive, can I?

The Female Pauper. No, no, mistress. Nobody can; she's far beyond the reach of help. But she's troubled in her mind. She says she has got something to tell which you must hear. She'll never die quiet till you come, mistress.

Mrs. Corney. Ptchah! These old women! They can't even die without annoying their betters! . . .

(She wraps herself in a shawl.)

. . . Will you wait here, Mr. Bumble? I'll be back presently . . .

(She follows the female pauper, scolding all the way.)

. . . Make haste, will you? Don't be all night hobbling up them stairs!

SCENE TWO
THE INFIRMARY

(In a bare garret-room, Old Sally is dying. There is another old woman watching by the bed; the parish apothecary's apprentice is standing by its foot, picking his teeth with a quill.)

The Apprentice *(As Mrs. Corney enters).* It's all U.P. here, Mrs. Corney.

Mrs. Corney. It is, is it, sir?

The Apprentice. If she lasts a couple of hours, I shall be surprised. It's a break-up of the system altogether. Is she dozing, old lady?

(The Old Woman stoops over the bed, to ascertain, and nods. The Apprentice drifts out.)

Mrs. Corney *(To the female pauper who has fetched her).* She might last two hours. Did you hear that? How long do you expect me to wait?

The Female Pauper. Not long, mistress. We have none of us long to wait for Death. Patience, patience! He'll be here soon enough for us all.

Mrs. Corney. Hold your tongue, you doting idiot! . . .

(She speaks to the old woman by the bed.)

. . . You, Martha, tell me; has she been in this way before?

The Old Woman. Often.

The Female Pauper. She'll never wake again but once—and mind, mistress, that won't be for long.

Mrs. Corney *(Snappishly).* Long or short, she won't find me here when she does wake; take care, both of you, you don't worry me again for nothing. It's no part of my duty to see all the old women in the house die—and what's more, I won't. Mind that, you impudent old harridans. If you make a fool of me again, I'll soon cure you, I warrant you!

(She is bouncing away, when there is a cry from the two women by the bed. **Old Sally** *raises herself upright and stretches out her arms.)*

Old Sally. Who's that?

The Old Woman. Hush, hush! Lie down, lie down!

Old Sally. I'll never lie down again alive! I will tell her! Come here! . . .

*(***Old Sally*** *clutches Mrs. Corney by the arm.)*

. . . Nearer! Let me whisper in your ear . . .

(She sees the two old women listening.)

. . . Turn them away. Make haste!

Mrs. Corney. Leave us, will you?

(The two old women move, protesting, to a place where they are apparently out of earshot.

Old Sally. Now listen to me. In this very room—in this very bed—I once nursed a pretty young creetur' that was brought into the house with her feet cut and bruised with walking, and all soiled with dust and blood. She gave birth to a boy, and died. Let me think—what was the year again?

Mrs. Corney *(Impatiently)*. Never mind the year! What about her?

Old Sally. Ay, what about . . what about . . . I know! I robbed her, so I did. She wasn't cold—I tell you, she wasn't cold, when I took it!

Mrs. Corney. Took what, for Goodness' sake?

Old Sally. The only thing she had. She wanted clothes to keep her warm, and food to eat, but she had kept it safe, and had it in her bosom. It was gold, I tell you! Rich gold, that might have saved her life!

Mrs. Corney. Gold! Go on, go on—yes—what of it? Who was the mother? When did this happen?

Old Sally. She charged me to keep it safe, and trusted me as the only woman about her. They would ha' treated that child better, if they had known it all!

Mrs. Corney. Known what? Speak?

Old Sally. The boy grew so like his mother that I could never forget it when I saw his face. Poor girl! Poor girl! She was so young, too! Such a gentle lamb! Wait! There's more to tell. I have not told you all, have I?

Mrs. Corney. No! No! Be quick, or it may be too late!

Old Sally. The mother, when the pains of death first came upon her, whispered in my ear that if her baby was born alive, and thrived, the day might come when it would not feel so much disgraced to hear its poor mother named. 'And Oh, kind Heaven!' she said, folding her thin hands together, 'whether it be boy or girl, raise up some friends for it in this troubled world, and take pity on a lonely, desolate child, abandoned to its mercy!'

Mrs. Corney. The boy's name?

Old Sally. They called him Oliver.

Mrs. Corney. Oliver!

Old Sally. The gold I stole was . . .

Mrs. Corney. Yes, yes—what?

(Mrs. Corney is bending eagerly over to hear Old Sally's reply when the old woman clutches the coverlet, mutters some

46

indistinct sounds in her throat, and falls lifeless. **Mrs. Corney** *takes a scrap of paper from the dead woman's hand, and hides it.)*

The Female Pauper *(Hurrying back).* Stone dead!

Mrs. Corney. And nothing to tell, after all.

(The **Matron** *walks carelessly back to her room, leaving the two crones to prepare for their dreadful duties.)*

SCENE THREE
THE MATRON'S ROOM

*(Mr. **Bumble** is holding his own, private inventory of the contents of the room when* **Mrs. Corney** *hurries in, throws herself in a breathless state on a chair by the fireside, and gasps for breath.)*

Mr. Bumble. Mrs. Corney, what is this, ma'am? Has anything happened, ma'am? Pray answer me; I'm on—on—

*(Mr. **Bumble**, in his alarm, cannot immediately think of the word 'tenterhooks'.)*

. . . on broken bottles, ma'am.

Mrs. Corney. Oh, Mr. Bumble! I have been so dreadfully put out!

Mr. Bumble. Put out, ma'am? Who has dared to . . . ? I know! This is them wicious paupers!

Mrs. Corney. It's dreadful to think of.!

(She shudders.)

Mr. Bumble. Then don't think of it, ma'am.

Mrs. Corney *(With a whimper).* I can't help it.

Mr. Bumble. Then take something, ma'am . . . A little of the wine?

Mrs. Corney. Not for the world! I couldn't . . . Oh! . . . The top shelf in the right-hand corner . . . Oh! . . .

(She points distractedly to a cupboard and then undergoes a convulsion from internal spasms. **Mr. Bumble** *rushes to the closet, brings back a pint green-glass bottle, fills a teacup with its contents and holds the cup to the lady's lips.)*

47

. . . I'm better now . . . It's peppermint. Try it! There's a little—
a little something else in it . . .

(Mr. Bumble tastes the medicine with a doubtful look; smacks his lips; takes another taste; and puts the cup down empty.)

. . . It's very comforting.

Mr. Bumble. Very much so indeed, ma'am . . .

(He draws a chair beside the matron)

. . . And now, ma'am, may I enquire what has happened to distress you?

Mrs. Corney. Nothing! I am a foolish, excitable, weak creetur.

Mr. Bumble *(Drawing his chair closer).* Not weak, ma'am. Are you a weak creetur, Mrs. Corney?

Mrs. Corney. We are all weak creeturs.

Mr. Bumble. So we are . . .

(Nothing is said, on either side, for a moment or two. By the end of that time, **Mr. Bumble's** *arm has become entwined with Mrs. Corney's apron-string.)*

. . . We are all weak creeturs . . .

*(***Mrs. Corney** *sighs.)*

. . . Don't sigh, Mrs. Corney.

Mrs. Corney. I can't help it.

(She sighs again.)

Mr. Bumble. This is a wery comfortable room, ma'am . . .

(He looks round.)

. . . Another room, and this, ma'am, would be a complete thing.

Mrs. Corney. It would be too much for one.

Mr. Bumble. But not for two, ma'am? Eh, Mrs. Corney? . . .

*(***Mrs. Corney** *with great propriety turns her head away. She releases her hand to get at her pocket-handerkerchief, but insensibly replaces it in that of Mr. Bumble.)*

. . . The Board allow you coals, don't they, Mrs. Corney?

(He affectionately presses her hand.)

Mrs. Corney. And candles.

(She slightly returns the pressure.)

Mr. Bumble. Coals, candles and house-rent free . . . Oh, Mrs. Corney, what an Angel you are! . . .

(Mrs. Corney sinks into Mr. Bumble's arms. Mr. Bumble imprints a passionate kiss on her chaste nose.)

. . . Such porochial perfection! You know that Mr. Slout is worse tonight, my fascinator?

Mrs. Corney. Yes.

Mr. Bumble. He can't live a week, the doctor says. He is the master of this establishment; his death will cause a wacancy; that wacancy must be filled up. Oh, Mrs. Corney, what a prospect this opens! What an opportunity for a jining of hearts and house-keepings!.. . .

(Mrs. Corney sobs.)

. . . The little word? The one little, little, little word, my blessed Corney?

Mrs. Corney. Ye-ye-yes!

Mr. Bumble. One more! Compose your darling feelings for only one more! When is it to come off?

(Mrs. Corney twice essays to speak, and twice fails. At last, she summons up courage and throws her arms round Mr. Bumble's neck.)

Mrs. Corney. It can come off as soon as you please, my love. You are an IR-RESISTIBLE DUCK!

SCENE FOUR
AT FAGIN'S

Oliver. In spite of my pleas and prayers, Fagin would not allow me to send any message to Mr. Brownlow, or to return the books, or in any other way to restore the old man's faith in me. Instead, I was kept a close prisoner at Fagin's for more than a month, being threatened, and cajoled, and told that I was

ungrateful whenever my captor had a few moments to spare
for hectoring me.

(**Fagin** *comes in, with* **Young Oliver**.*)*

Fagin. You was lonely, and hungry, and had nowhere to go when I
took you in, is not that right, my dear? If it hadn't been for me,
you might have perished with hunger. Well, what do you want
to run away from your wery good friends for? I can't understand
it, I just can't understand it. But you won't be trying it again,
will you, my darling? Else you may finish up like a young lad I
once took in here—such a nice, good-looking young fellow—but
was he grateful? Did he appreciate what I was doing for him?
He . . .

(**Fagin** *lowers his voice.)*

. . . He tried to peach on us, my dear. He tried to blab on the
friends that had looked after him, that had filled his stomach
and had given him a soft pillow for his head . . .

(**Fagin** *sighs deeply, so that tears well into his kind old eyes.)*

. . . Well, there was only one thing we could do, of course. We
had to see that he was taken care of. There's such a thing as
Crown Evidence, my dear—you may not have come across the
words yet, but you will, you will . . . 'Crown Evidence', just you
remember them . . .

(*He sighs again, and shakes his head as he remembers the
unfortunate young man who was so very disloyal.)*

. . . They took him out one morning, just when Newgate Clock
was striking eight. It isn't pleasant when they come for you that
early, my dear. You've hardly had time to digest your breakfast
in comfort before there's a knock on your door, and Mr. Ketch
is outside, with his assistants, and the Chaplain. He's a rough man
is Mr. Jack Ketch, my dearest . . .

Young Oliver *(Shuddering)*. Don't!

Fagin. He ties you up, so that his men can put you just where he wants
you, on his trap.

Young Oliver. Don't! Don't! Don't!

Fagin. And then he puts a horrid, stuffy black bandage over your
eyes . . .

Young Oliver. O-o-o-o-h!

(With a long, shuddering cry **Young Oliver** *runs away from Fagin.)*

Fagin. We won't have much more trouble from that quarter, I imagine. He's a sensible child, is young Oliver. He'll soon learn what is good for his health and what isn't.

*(***Bill Sikes** *comes up from the street, followed by* **Nancy.***)*

Bill Sikes. Well!

Fagin. Well, my dear—Ah, Nancy!

Nancy. Cold, Fagin.

Fagin. It is cold, Nancy dear. It seems to go right through one.

Bill Sikes. It must be a piercer if it finds its way through your heart. Give him something to drink, Nancy. Burn my body, make haste! It's enough to turn a man ill, to see his lean old carcase shivering in that way, like a ugly ghost just riz from the grave.

*(***Nancy** *produces a large bottle of brandy from under her shawl and pours out a glass of it for Fagin.)*

Fagin *(Putting down the glass after just setting his lips to it).* Quite enough, quite, thankye, Bill.

Bill Sikes. What? You're afraid of our getting the better of you, are you? Ugh . . .

(The burglar seizes the glass and throws its contents away. Then he fills it again, and tosses down the second glassful.)

. . . There! Now I'm ready.

Fagin. For business?

Bill Sikes. For business. So say what you've got to say.

Fagin. About the crib at Chertsey, Bill?

Bill Sikes. Yus. Wot about it?

Fagin. Ah, you know what I mean, my dear. When is it to be done, Bill, eh? When is it to be done? Such plate, my dear, such plate!

*(***Fagin** *rubs his hands and elevates his eyebrows in a rapture of anticipation.)*

Bill Sikes *(Coldly).* It ain't goin' to be done at all.

Fagin. Ain't goin' to be done at all?

51

Bill Sikes. No. Leastways, it can't be a put-up job, as we expected.

Fagin *(Turning pale with anger).* Then it hasn't been properly gone about. Don't tell me!

Bill Sikes. But I will tell yer. Who are you that's not to be told? I tells yer that Toby Crackit 'as been 'anging abaht the place for a fortnight, and 'e can't get none of the servants into a line.

Fagin *(With a deep sigh).* It's a sad thing, my dear, to lose so much when we had set our hearts upon it.

Bill Sikes. So it is. Worse luck! . . .

(He looks furtively at Fagin.)

. . . Fagin! Is it worth fifty shiners extra if it's safely done from the outside?

Fagin. Yes!

Bill Sikes. Is that a bargain?

Fagin. Yes, my dear, yes!

Bill Sikes. Then let it come off as soon as you like. Toby and me were over the garden-wall the night afore last, a-soundin' the panels of the doors and shutters. The crib's barred up at night like a jail; but there's one part we can crack, safe and softly.

Fagin. Which is that, Bill?

Bill Sikes. Why, as you cross the lawn . . .

(He looks hard at Fagin.)

. . . Never you mind which part it is. You can't do it without me, I know; but it's best to be on the safe side when one deals with coves like you.

Fagin. As you like, my dear, as you like. Is there no help wanted, but yours and Toby's?

Bill Sikes. None, 'cept a centre-bit and a boy. The first we've both got; the second you must find us.

Fagin. A boy! Oh, then it's a panel, eh?

Bill Sikes. Never mind wot it is! I wants a boy, and 'e mustn't be a big'un. Lord! If I'd only got that young boy of Ned, the chimbley-sweeper's! 'E kept 'im small on purpose, and let 'im out by the job. But the farver gits lagged; and then the Juvenile Delinquent Society comes an' tikes the boy away from a trade where 'e was earnin' money, teaches 'im to read and write, and in time makes a happrentice on 'im; And so they goes on! If they'd got money enough, we shouldn't have half-a-dozen boys left in the 'ole tride in a year or two.

Fagin. No more we should, no more we should . . .

(An idea strikes him.)

. . . Bill! What about Oliver?

Bill Sikes. Oliver? What Oliver?

Fagin. Young Oliver Twist! He's the boy for you, my dear!

Bill Sikes. Wot! 'Im?

Fagin. Take him, Bill. I would, if I was in your place. He mayn't be so much up as any of the others, but that's not what you want if he's only to open a door for you.

Bill Sikes. Would 'e be sife?

Fagin. I know he is, now. He's been in good training these last few weeks, and it's time he began to work for his bread. Besides, the others are all too big.

Bill Sikes *(Ruminating).* 'E's just the size I wants.

Fagin. And will do everything you want, Bill, my dear. He can't help himself. That is, if you frighten him enough.

Bill Sikes. Frighten him! It'll be no sham frightening, mind yer. If there's anyfink bent abaht 'im when we once gits into the work you won't see him alive again, Fagin. You think on that, before you sends 'im.

Fagin. I've thought of it all. I've had my eye on him, my dears—close, close. Once let him feel that he is one of us; once fill his mind with the idea that he has been a thief; and he's our's! Ours for his life. And, he'd better be. He knows too much about us now. He can shop us all if he tries giving leg-bail again. But it'll be quite enough for my power over him that he's been in a robbery. That's all I want. It couldn't have come about better.

Nancy. When's the job to be done, Bill?

Fagin. Ah, to be sure. When is it to be done, Bill?

Bill Sikes. I planned with Toby, the night arter tomorrer. If 'e 'eard nothink from me to the contrairy.

Fagin. Good. There's no moon.

Bill Sikes. No.

Fagin. It's all been arranged about bringing off the swag, is it? . . .

*(*Bill Sikes *nods.)*

. . . And about . . .

Bill Sikes. Oh, ah, it's all planned. Never mind particulars. You go and git that boy. I wants ter git off the stones afore daybreak.

(Fagin goes to fetch Young Oliver.)

Fagin. Come, my dear, you're going to go on a nice little journey into the country with Mr. Sikes.

Young Oliver *(Anxiously).* To—to—stop there, Sir?

Fagin. No, no, my dear. Not to stop there. We shouldn't like to lose you. Don't be afraid, Oliver, you shall come back to us again. Ha! Ha! Ha! We won't be so cruel as to send you away, my dear, Oh no! No! . . .

(He looks round furtively.)

. . . I suppose you want to know what you are going with Bill for, eh, my dear? . . .

(Young Oliver nods his head.)

. . . Why, do you think?

Young Oliver. Indeed I don't know, sir.

Fagin. Bah! Wait till Bill tells you, then . . .

(He hesitates, and then puts a warning hand on Young Oliver's arm.)

. . . Take heed, Oliver! Take heed! He's a rough man, and thinks nothing of blood when his own is up. Whatever falls out, say nothing; and do what he bids you. Mind!

(With a final admonitory wag of his forefinger, Fagin leaves Young Oliver alone.)

Oliver. But Bill's instructions, when they came, were not particularly informative.

Bill Sikes. Come 'ere young 'un, and let me read you a lectur', which is as well got over at once . . .

(Young Oliver stands in front of Bill Sikes, who takes up a pocket-pistol.)

. . . Now, first: do you know wot this is? . . .

(Young Oliver nods his head.)

. . . Well, then, look here. This is powder; that 'ere's a bullet; and this is a little bit of a old 'at, fer waddin' . . .

(Bill Sikes proceeds to load the pistol, with great nicety and deliberation.)

. . . Now it's loaded.

Young Oliver. Yes, I see it is, Sir.

Bill Sikes. Well, if you speak a word when you're out o'doors wi' me, except when I speaks ter you, that loading will be in yer 'ead without notice. So, if you do make up yer mind to speak without leave, say yer prayers first . . .

(Bill Sikes scowls at Young Oliver to increase the effect of his warning.)

. . . As near as I know, there ain't anybody as would be askin very partickler arter you, if you was disposed of; so I needn't take this devil-and-all of trouble to explain matters to yer, if it warn't fer your own good. D'ye hear me? . . .

(Young Oliver nods.)

. . . And now, let Nancy take 'ee off and give 'ee a good bellyful of scoff before we sets out. It'll be quite a long time, before we're both back.

Nancy *(As she takes Young Oliver off for food).* You'll be all right, my dear, as long as you don't cross him. If you do, 'e'll stop you telling tales for ever arterwards, and 'e'll take 'is chance of swingin' for it. C'mon. I expect you're 'ungry.

Oliver. But you didn't shoot me, did you, Bill Sikes?

Bill Sikes. Nah. That wasn't the way it worked out at all. When we got to the crib we was goin' ter crack, I showed you a little lattice window, remember?

Oliver. I remember.

Bill Sikes. And Flash Toby and I put yer through it, remember that too?

Oliver. How could I forget? You told me you'd give me a crack on the head with your gun if I didn't do exactly as you told me.

Bill Sikes. And do yer wonder? Yer was prayin' ter all the Bright

55

Angels in 'Eaven ter 'ave mercy on yer. We only wanted yer to undo the street door and let us in.

Oliver. But I didn't get a chance, did I? Almost as soon as I got my feet on the scullery floor I dropped the lantern I was carrying . . .

Bill Sikes. That brought the two men servants to the top of the stairs, blast yer . . .

Oliver. Everything swam in front of my eyes . . .

Bill Sikes. There was a flash . . .

Oliver. A loud noise . . .

Bill Sikes. It knocked Toby and me flat backwards, tip over tail . . .

Oliver. There was smoke everywhere . . .

Bill Sikes. But we got yer by the collar, and dragged yer back . . .

Oliver. I can remember the loud ringing of a bell, mingled with the noise of firearms . . .

Bill Sikes. There was men shoutin', everywhere . . .

Oliver. And I felt as if I was being carried over uneven ground at a rapid pace.

Bill Sikes. You was. By me.

Oliver. But then the noises grew confused in the distance.

Bill Sikes. You was feelin' faint, more as like. I'ad you 'ead dahnwards over me shoulder.

Oliver. And I remember no more.

Bill Sikes. That's 'cos I 'ad to drop yer dahn in a dry ditch when the chase got too 'ot. Yer was like deff itself, when I left yer.

Oliver. But, somehow, I found my way back to the house you had taken me to rob. I pushed against the garden-gate, tottered across the lawn, climbed the steps, knocked faintly on the door, and, my whole strength failing me, sank down against one of the pillars of the little portico.

Bill Sikes. By that time, o'course, Toby and me was 'arf way back to London.

(Bill lurches off.)

SCENE FIVE
AT THE WORKHOUSE, AGAIN

*(Mr. Bumble comes in and sits down in the Matron's parlour.
He rests his eyes moodily on the cheerless grate, though he
raises them occasionally to look at a paper fly-cage that dangles
from the ceiling. The sight depresses him deeply, reminding him,
as it does, of his present unhappy condition.)*

Mr. Bumble *(With a sigh).* And tomorrow two months it was done!
It seems a hage . . .

*(He closes his eyes for a moment, as if he can bear no longer
the sight of the captured flies.)*

. . . I sold myself for six teaspoons, a pair of sugar-tongs, and a
milk-pot; with a small quantity of second-hand furniture, and
twenty pound in money. I went very reasonable. Cheap, dirt
cheap!

Mrs. Bumble *(Materializing almost from nowhere).* Cheap! You would
have been dear at any price; and dear enough I paid for you,
Lord above knows that!

Mr. Bumble *(Turning suddenly).* Mrs. Bumble, ma'am!

Mrs. Bumble. Well?

Mr. Bumble. Have the goodness to look at me.

Mrs. Bumble. Look at you? Hah! Oh, hah! . . .

*(Mr. Bumble, finding that his pauper-quelling eye is powerless
against Mrs. Bumble, relapses into gloom.)*

. . . Well? Are you going to sit snoring there all day?

Mr. Bumble. I am going to sit here, as long as I think proper, ma'am;
and although I was *not* snoring, I shall snore, gape, sneeze,
laugh, or cry, as the humour strikes me; such being my
prerogative.

Mrs. Bumble *(With ineffable contempt).* Your prerogative!

Mr. Bumble. I said the word, ma'am. The prerogative of a man is to
command.

Mrs. Bumble. And what's the prerogative of a woman, in the name of
Goodness?

Mr. Bumble. To obey, ma'am. Your late unfortunate husband should have taught it you; and then, perhaps, he might have been alive now. I wish he was, poor man! . . .

(Mrs. Bumble sees that the decisive moment has now arrived, and that a blow struck for mastership at this point must necessarily be final and conclusive. She drops into a chair, accuses Mr. Bumble with a loud scream of being a hard-hearted brute, and falls into a paroxysm of tears.)

Mr. Bumble *(Whose heart is water-proof).* Cry on, my sweetest. I beg you, cry your hardest. The practice is looked on, they say, has being 'ighly conducive to 'ealth. It opens the lungs . . .

*(A howl, from **Mrs. Bumble**.)*

. . . It washes the countenance, it exercises the eyes, and softens down the temper. So cry away, me loving poppet, cry away.

*(**Mr. Bumble** puts on his hat at a rakish angle and, having asserted his superiority, and the superiority of all males, so effectively, he saunters towards the door.*

*But **Mrs. Bumble** has only tried tears because they are less troublesome, for her, than a manual assault. Before Mr. Bumble can escape she sends his hat flying suddenly to the opposite end of the room. Then she clasps him tightly round the throat with one hand and inflicts condign punishment on him, in a highly expert way, with the other. Finally, she pushes him over a chair.)*

Mrs. Bumble. Prerogative! Prerogative! Just mention that word again if you dare! And now, get up! And take yourself away from here, unless you want me to do something desperate! . . .

*(**Mr. Bumble** rises with a very rueful countenance, wondering what something desperate may be. He picks up his hat and looks towards the door.)*

. . . Are you going?

Mr. Bumble. Certainly, my dear, certainly. I didn't intend to . . . I'm going, my dear! You are so very violent, that really I . . .

*(**Mrs. Bumble** steps hastily forward to replace the carpet, which has been kicked up in the scuffle. **Mr. Bumble** immediately darts to a position safely out of her range.*

*While he is recovering his breath, and his equilibrium, he is approached by a mysterious stranger. It is **Mr. Monks,** whom we last saw at Fagin's.)*

Mr. Monks. Excuse me, sir, do you happen to be the beadle here?

Mr. Bumble. I was, young man, I was. The Porochial Beadle. But now I am the Master of the Workhouse. The Master of the Workhouse, young man!

Mr. Monks. You have an eye to your own interest, I doubt not? Don't scruple to answer freely, man.

Mr. Bumble. I suppose, a married man is not more averse to turning an honest penny when he can than a single one. Porochial officers are not so well paid that they can afford to refuse any extra fee when it comes to them in a civil and proper manner.

Mr. Monks. I want some information from you. I don't ask you to give it for nothing, slight as it is. Put up that, to begin with . . .

(He hands two sovereigns to **Mr. Bumble***, who examines them scrupulously to see that they are genuine, and then puts them with much satisfaction in his waistcoat-pocket.)*

. . . Carry your memory back—let me see—twelve years last winter.

Mr. Bumble. It's a long time . . . Very good, I've done it.

Mr. Monks. The scene, the workhouse.

Mr. Bumble. Good!

Mr. Monks. And the time, night.

Mr. Bumble. Yes.

Mr. Monks. The place, the crazy hole where miserable drabs give birth to puling children for the parish to rear.

Mr. Bumble *(Not quite following).* The lying-in room, I suppose?

Mr. Monks. Yes. A boy was born there.

Mr. Bumble. A many boys.

(He shakes his head despondingly.)

Mr. Monks. I speak of one: a meek-looking, pale-faced boy, who was apprenticed down here to a coffin-maker, and who afterwards ran away to London, as it is supposed.

Mr. Bumble. Why, you mean Oliver! Young Twist! I remember him, of course. There wasn't an obstinater young rascal . . .

Mr. Monks. It's not of him I want to hear. It's of a woman; the woman that nursed his mother. Where is she?

Mr. Bumble. Where is she? It would be hard to tell. There's no midwifery there, whichever place she's gone to.

Mr. Monks. What do you mean?

Mr. Bumble. She died last winter.

(**Mr. Monks** *draws in his breath sharply.*)

Mr. Monks. It's no great matter. And now, I have a long way to go.

Mr. Bumble. Wait! My wife . . . the Workhouse Master's wife . . . She was with Old Sally, if I remember haright, on the evening she died. I have reason to believe that Old Sally may have told her something.

(*He walks across to* Mrs. Bumble, *who has been well aware of what has been going on.*)

. . . My dear . . .

(*He whispers in her ear, then she nods her head, then he goes across to* **Mr.** Monks *and leads him to Mrs. Bumble.*)

Mr. Monks. Madam, I believe you were with a certain old woman of this workhouse when she died . . .

(**Mrs. Bumble** *inclines her head.*)

Your husband tells me that she may have told you something . . .

Mrs. Bumble. About the mother of a certain boy we once had here. Yes.

Mr. Monks. The first question is, of what nature was her communication?

Mrs. Bumble. That's the second question. The first is, what may the communication be worth?

Mr. Monks. Hah! There may be money's worth to get, eh?

Mrs. Bumble. Perhaps there may.

Mr. Monks. Something that was taken from her? Something that she wore? Something . . .

Mrs. Bumble *(Interrupting).* You had better make me an offer. I've heard enough already to tell me you're the man I ought to talk to. What's it worth to you?

Mr. Monks. It may be nothing; it may be twenty ponnds. Speak out, and let me know which.

Mrs. Bumble. Give me five-and-twenty pounds in gold, and I'll tell you all I know. Not before.

Mr. Monks. Five and twenty pounds!

Mrs. Bumble. I spoke as plainly as I could. It's not a large sum, either.

Mr. Monks. Not a large sum for a paltry secret that may be nothing when it's told?

Mrs. Bumble. You can easily take it away again. I am but a woman; alone here; and unprotected.

Mr. Bumble. Not alone, my dear, nor unprotected neither . . .

(His teeth chatter as he speaks.)

. . . I am here, my dear. And, besides, Mr. Monks is too much of a gentleman to attempt any violence on porochial persons. Mr. Monks is aware that I am not a young man, my dear, and also that I am a little run to seed, as I may say; but he has heerd: I say I have no doubt Mr. Monks has heerd, my dear: that I am a very determined officer, with very uncommon strength, if I'm once roused. I only want a little rousing, that's all.

Mrs. Bumble. You're a fool; and you'd better hold your tongue.

(Mr. Monks produces a canvas bag and counts out twenty five sovereigns.)

Mr. Monks. There are the sovereigns. Now, let's hear your story.

Mrs. Bumble. When this woman, that we called Old Sally, died, she and I were alone.

Mr. Monks. Good. Go on.

Mrs. Bumble. She spoke of a young creature who had brought a child into the world some years before; not merely in the same room, but in the same bed in which she then lay dying. The child was the boy you named. The mother, Old Sally had robbed.

Mr. Monks. In life?

Mrs. Bumble. In death. She stole from the corpse something that the dying mother had prayed her, with her last breath, to keep for the infant's sake.

Mr. Monks. She sold it? Did she sell it? Where? When? To whom? How long before?

Mrs. Bumble. When Old Sally died, I found in her hand a scrap of dirty paper.

Mr. Monks. Which contained?

Mrs. Bumble. Nothing. It was a pawnbroker's ticket.

Mr. Monks. For what?

Mrs. Bumble. She must have kept the trinkets she took from the dying woman for some time, in the hope of turning them to better account. Then, she must have pawned them. Each year, she must have saved or scraped enough money together to pay the pawnbroker's interest, and prevent its running out; so that if anything came of the matter the trinkets could still be redeemed. Nothing had come of it; and, as I tell you, she died with the scrap of paper, all worn and tattered, in her hand. The time was out in two days; I thought something might one day come of it, too; and so I redeemed the pledge.

Mr. Monks. Where is it now?

Mrs. Bumble. There!

*(She hands across a small kid bag, which **Mr. Monks** pounces upon, and tears open.)*

Mr. Monks *(As he inspects the contents of the bag).* A gold locket . . . Yes! . . . A plain gold wedding ring . . . Yes! . . . With 'Agnes' engraved on the inside, and a blank left for the surname . . . Then follows the date . . . And is this all?

Mrs. Bumble. All. Is it what you expected to get from me?

Mr. Monks. It is . . .

(He puts the bag carefully away in his pocket.)

. . . And now, we can have nothing more to say, and may break up our pleasant party.

SCENE SIX
AT FAGIN'S

(Darkness.
There is a faint glimmer of a lantern, and then a low whistle.
The whistle is repeated.)

The Artful Dodger *(In a whisper).* Now then?

Toby Crackit *(In a whisper).* Plummy and slam!

The Artful Dodger. Come on in. Wait there.

*(**The Artful Dodger** moves away and whispers mysteriously to Fagin.)*

Fagin. What, alone?

The Artful Dodger. Yus.

Fagin. Where is he?

The Artful Dodger. Out there.

Fagin. Bring him in. Hush! Quiet, Charley! Gently, Tom! Scarce! Scarce!

(The boys, hidden in the shadows, disperse.)

Toby Crackit. How are you, Faguey? . . .

*(*Fagin *grips him by the collar.)*

. . . Don't look at me in that way, man. All in good time. I can't talk business till I've eat and drank, so produce some scoffer, will yer? I ain't 'ad nuffin, 'ardly, these three days and nights.

Fagin. The Dodger 'll get you some grub presently. Here's some gin, my dearest. Get that inside you. Then you'll be ready for talking.

*(*Toby Crackit *drinks.)*

Toby Crackit. Tchah! That's better. Now, first and foremost, Faguey, how's Bill?

Fagin *(A scream).* WHAT?

Toby Crackit. Why, you don't mean to say . . .

Fagin. Mean? Where are they? Sikes and the boy! Where are they? Where have they been? Where are they hiding? Why have they not been here?

Toby Crackit *(Faintly).* The crack failed.

Fagin. Failed?

Toby Crackit. They fired and hit the boy. We cut over the fields at the back, with him between us . . . straight as the crow flies . . . through 'edge and ditch. They gave chase. Damme! The whole country was awake, and the dogs upon us.

Fagin. The boy?

Toby Crackit. Bill 'ad 'im on 'is back, and scudded like the wind. We stopped to take 'im between us; 'is 'ead 'ung down, and 'e was cold. They were close upon our 'eels; every man for 'imself, and each from the gallows! We parted company, and left the youngster lying in a ditch. Alive or dead, that's all I know about 'im . . .

63

(Fagin utters a loud yell, and wrings his hands.)

. . . Though I did 'ear tell, in two of the ale'ouses I stopped at, that the boy 'ad gone back to the crib, and 'ad been taken in, and was being looked arter by the fambly.

Fagin. Oy! . . Oy! . . Oy! . . Oh, why should this happen to me? . . .

(He hears the soft sound of a footstep.)

. . . Go through to the back, my dearest. The Dodger will give you your grub . . .

(Fagin has hardly ushered Toby Crackit out, before Monks appears, in the other doorway.)

Monks. Fagin!

Fagin *(Turning quickly round)*. Ah! Is that . . .

Monks. Yes! I have been waiting for you for hours. Where the devil have you been?

Fagin. On your business, my dear. On your business all night.

Monks *(With a sneer)*. Oh, of course! Well; and what's come of it?

Fagin. Nothing good.

Monks. Nothing bad, I hope? . . .

(He looks round.)

. . . Can anyone hear?

Fagin. Not a living soul. Toby Crackit's in the back room having his grub, and the boys are with him.

Monks. And Oliver?

Fagin. Oliver's at Chertsey, still. I sent him out on a crack with Bill Sikes, and the crack failed. They scarpered, across country, but Bill had to drop the boy when the pace got too hot. Flash Toby Crackit has heard he went back to the crib. Taken in and made much of, he said. It was the talk of the ale-houses as he came through.

Monks. Damnation to you, Fagin! . . .

(He grips Fagin by the collar and shakes him as a dog shakes a rat.)

. . . Damnation to you. Why in hell's name couldn't you have kept him here among the rest, and made a sneaking, snivelling pickpocket of him at once?

Fagin *(With a shrug)*. Only hear him!

Monks. Why, do you mean to say you couldn't have done it, if you had chosen? Haven't you done it with other boys, scores of times? If you had had patience for a twelvemonth, at most, couldn't you have got him convicted, and sent safely out of the kingdom; perhaps for life?

Fagin. Whose turn would that have served, my dear?

Monks. Mine.

Fagin. But not mine, He would have become of use to me, my dear, but his hand was not in. I had nothing to frighten him with; which we always must have in the beginning, or we labour in vain. What could I do? Send him out with the Dodger, and Charley? We had enough of that at first, my dear; I trembled for us all. But do not worry. I got him back once, by means of the girl. I'll get him back again, or my name's not Fagin.

Monks. You'd better, Fagin, or I'll break every bone in your nasty body, d'you understand? There, take these papers, and hide 'em . . .

(He hands a small bundle of letters to Fagin.)

. . . the only other proofs of that boy's identity now lie at the bottom of the river, and the old hag that took them from the mother is rotting in her coffin. His money is mine, Fagin, mine! But I won't feel safe until . . .

(He starts.)

. . . Fire this infernal den! What's that?

Fagin. What? Where?

Monks. Yonder! The shadow! I saw the shadow of a woman, in a cloak and bonnet, pass along the wainscot like a breath!

Fagin. It's your fancy!

Monks. I swear I saw it! It was bending forward when I saw it first. When I spoke, it darted away!

Fagin. Besides ourselves, there's not a creature in the house except Toby and the boys; and they're safe enough. See here! . . .

*(He draws **Monks** forward to inspect the shadowy recesses at the head of the stairs.)*

. . . Come, we'll go to Bill's ken. He may be back there, by now. He'll know how to get Young Oliver back, if anyone does.

As long, my dear, as you're ready to make it worth his while.

(As soon as Fagin and Monks have gone, **Nancy** *comes out from the dark corner in which she has been eaves dropping.)*

Nancy. I'll go! I'll go to Chertsey! I'll warn them! I know where their crib is! No, no. That would be dangerous, to go there. I know what—I'll send 'em a message. I'll ask 'em to meet me somewhere— on London Bridge, say—on Sunday, between eleven and midnight. I'd rather that boy was dead, and out of harm's way, than be brought back to this place again, alive.

SCENE SEVEN
BILL SIKES' KEN AT BETHNAL GREEN

Oliver. But when the night came on which Nancy had arranged to meet the kind people who were giving me a home, she did not find it easy to keep the appointment.

(A clock strikes eleven. **Bill Sikes** *comes in, with* **Fagin.***)*

Bill Sikes. An hour this side of midnight. Dark and 'eavy it is, too. A good night for business, this.

Fagin. Ah! What a pity, Bill my dear, that there's none quite ready to be done.

Bill Sikes. You're right for once. It's a pity, for I'm in the humour, too. We must make up for lost time when . . .

*(***Nancy*** *comes in. She is wearing a bonnet.)*

. . . Hallo! Nance! Where's the gal going to at this time of night?

Nancy. Not far.

Bill Sikes. What answer's that? Where are you going?

Nancy. I say, not far.

Bill Sikes. And I say where? Do you hear me?

Nancy. I don't know where.

Bill Sikes. Then I do. You're going nowhere. Sit down.

Nancy. I'm not well. I told you that before. I want a breath of air.

Bill Sikes. Then put yer 'ead out of the winder.

Nancy. There's not enough there. I want it in the street.

Bill Sikes. Then you won't 'ave it . . .

(He locks the door, removes the key, and pulls the bonnet off her head.)

. . . There. Now stop quietly where yer are, will yer?

Nancy. It's not such a matter as a bonnet would keep me. What do you mean, Bill? Do you know what you are doing?

Bill Sikes. Know what I'm . . . Oh!

(He turns to Fagin.)

. . . The wench is out of 'er senses, or she dursn't talk to me in that way.

Nancy. You'll drive me on to something desperate. Let me go, will you? . . . This minute! . . . This instant!

Bill Sikes. No!

Nancy. Tell him to let me go. Fagin. He had better. It'll be better for him. Do you hear me?

Bill Sikes. Hear you? Aye! And if I hear you for 'arf a minute longer I'll tear some of that screaming voice aht. Wot 'as come over you, you jade? Wot is it?

Nancy. Let me go! Bill, let me go; you don't know what you are doing. You don't indeed. For only one hour—do—do!

Bill Sikes. The girl's stark, raving mad. Git up off the floor!

Nancy. Not till you lets me go . . . Not till you lets me go . . . Never . . . Never!

*(She screams. **Bill Sikes** watches his opportunity, then he pinions her hands and drags her, struggling and wrestling by the way, into an adjoining room. Her moans can be heard until **Bill Sikes** returns.)*

Bill Sikes. That's settled 'er fer a bit. I've strapped 'er to the bedpost. Wot a precious strange gal she is!

Fagin *(Thoughtfully)*. You may say that, Bill. You may say that.

Bill Sikes. Wot did she tike it inter 'er 'ead to go out tonight for, do yer think? Wot does it mean?

Fagin. Obstinacy; woman's obstinacy, I suppose, my dear.

Bill Sikes. I suppose it is. I thought I 'ad tamed 'er but she's as bad as ever . . .

(There is an extra-loud scream from Nancy.)

. . . Come on, let's go and 'ave another look at 'er. Stuff 'er gob-'ole if she don't pipe dahn.

(Bill Sikes and Fagin go out.)

SCENE EIGHT
OUTSIDE AN ALE-HOUSE

Oliver. Fagin's suspicions were throughly aroused by Nancy's intransigeance, and he determined to have her watched—if possible, by some one she could not conceivably recognize. He found a suitable candidate quite by chance, in the person of Noah Claypole, who had just arrived in London with Charlotte, and the contents of Mr. Sowerberry's till.

(Noah Claypole and Charlotte, with a bundle each, and a glass and a half of ale, sit down at an outdoor table to continue a conversation.)

Noah Claypole. So I means ter be a gentleman. No more jolly old coffins, Charlotte, but a gentleman's life for me: and if yer like yer shall be a lady.

Charlotte. I should like that well enough, dear. But tills ain't to be emptied every day, and people to get clear off after it.

Noah Claypole. Tills be blowed! There's more things besides tills to be emptied.

Charlotte. What do you mean?

Noah Claypole. Pockets, women's ridicules, houses, mail-coaches, banks!

Charlotte. But you can't do all that, dear.

Noah Claypole. I shall look out to get into company with them as can. They'll be able to make us useful some way or another. Why, you yourself are worth fifty women; I never see such a precious sly and deceitful creetur as yer can be when I lets yer.

Charlotte. Lor, how nice it is to hear you say so!

(She imprints a kiss on Noah Claypole's ugly face)

Noah Claypole. There, that'll do: don't yer be too affectionate, in case I'm cross with yer.

*(As **Noah Claypole** disengages himself, **Fagin** approaches the table.)*

Fagin. A pleasant night, Sir, but cool for the time of year. From the country, I see, Sir?

Noah Claypole. How do yer see that?

Fagin. We have not so much dust as that in London.

(He points to the travellers' shoes, and then to their bundles.)

Noah Claypole. Yer a sharp feller. Ha! Ha! Only hear that, Charlotte.

Fagin *(Sinking his voice to a confidential whisper).* Why, one need be sharp in this town, my dear, and that's the truth . . . The . . .

(He taps Noah Claypole's glass.)

. . . The price of porter!

Noah Claypole. Good stuff that.

Fagin. Dear! Very dear! A man need be always emptying a till, or a pocket, or a woman's reticule, or a house, or a mail-coach, or a bank, if he drinks it regularly . . .

*(**Noah Claypole** looks at him with a countenance of ashy paleness and excessive terror.)*

. . . Don't mind me, my dear! Ha! Ha! It was lucky it was only me that heard you by chance. It was very lucky it was only me.

Noah Claypole. I didn't take it. It was all her doing. Yer've got it now, Charlotte, yer know yer have.

Fagin. No matter who's got it, or who did it, my dear . . .

(He shoots a hawk-like glance at Charlotte, and then at the two bundles.)

. . . I'm that way inclined myself, and I like you for it. In fact, I wouldn't mind putting you in the way of a little bit of business where your talents could be usefully employed . . .

(He leans over the table.)

. . . I would like you to do a piece of work for me that needs great care and caution.

Noah Claypole. I say! Don't yer go shoving me into danger, or sending me near any of them police offices. That don't suit me, that don't; and so I tell yer.

Fagin. There's not the smallest danger in it . . . not the very smallest. It's only to dodge a woman.

Noah Claypole. An old woman?

Fagin. A young one.

Noah Claypole. I can do that pretty well, I know. I was a regular cunning sneak when I was at school. What am I to dodge her for? Not to . . .

Fagin. Not to do anything, but to tell me where she goes, who she sees, and, if possible, what she says; to remember the street, if it is a street, or the house, if it is a house; and to bring me back all the information you can.

Noah Claypole. What'll yer give me?

Fagin. If you do it well, a pound, my dear. One pound! And that's what I never gave yet for any job of work where there wasn't valuable consideration to be gained.

Noah Claypole. Who is she?

Fagin. One of my . . . friends.

Noah Claypole. Oh Lor! Yer doubtful of her, are yer?

Fagin. She has found out some new friends, my dear, and I must know who they are.

Noah Claypole. I see. Just to have the pleasure of knowing them, if they're respectable people, eh? Ha! Ha! Ha! I'm yer man.

Fagin. I knew you would be.

Noah Claypole. Of course, of course. Where is she? Where am I to wait for her? Where am I to go?

Fagin. All that, my dear, you shall hear from me. I'll point her out at the proper time. Just step this way, will you, and leave the rest to me?

SCENE NINE
AT FAGIN'S

(It is nearly two hours before daybreak, and **Fagin** *sits watching in his lair. At first it is too dark for us to see him. Then, as four o'clock strikes, we can dimly perceive him as he sits crouched*

70

over his cold hearth, wrapped in an old torn coverlet.
Stretched on a mattress on the floor we can see **Noah Claypole**
fast asleep. There is a gentle knock at the street door.)

Fagin. At last . . .

(He wipes his dry and fevered mouth.)

. . . At last!

(He goes to the door, and returns with **Bill Sikes,** *who is*
muffled to the chin, and carrying a bundle.)

Bill Sikes. There! . . .

(The robber lays the bundle on the table.)

. . . Take care of that, and do the most you can with it. It's
been trouble enough to get: I thought I should have been here
three hours ago . . .

*(***Fagin*** *locks the bundle away, without taking his eyes off Bill*
Sikes for an instant.)

. . . Wot now? Wot do you look at a man so for? . . .

*(***Fagin*** *raises his right hand, but his passion is so great that he*
has lost the power of speech.)

. . . Damme! He's gone mad. I must look to myself here.

Fagin. No, no . . . It's not . . . You're not the person, Bill. I've no . . .
no fault to find with you.

Bill Sikes. Oh, you haven't, haven't you? . . .

(He ostentatiously passes a pistol into a more convenient pocket.)

. . . That's lucky for one of us. Which one that is, don't matter.

Fagin. I've got that to tell you, Bill, will make you worse than me.

Bill Sikes. Aye? Tell away! Look sharp, or Nance will think I'm lost.

Fagin. Lost! She has pretty well settled that in her own mind already.

Bill Sikes. *(Clutching Fagin's coat collar in his huge hand and shaking*
him soundly). Speak, will you! Open your mouth and say wot
you've got to say in plain words. Out with it, you thundering
old cur, out with it!

Fagin. Suppose that lad that's lying there . . .

*(***Bill Sikes*** *turns to look at Noah Claypole.)*

71

Bill Sikes. Well?

Fagin. Suppose that lad was to peach . . . to blow upon us all . . . first seeking out the right folks for the purpose, and then having a meeting with 'em in the street to paint our likenesses, describe every mark that they might know us by, and the crib where we might be most easily taken. Suppose he was to do all this, and besides to blow upon a plant we've all been in, more or less, of his own fancy; not grabbed, trapped, tried, earwigged by the parson and brought to it on bread and water, but of his own fancy; to please his own taste; stealing out at nights to find those most interested against us, and peaching to them. Do you hear me? . . .

(His eyes flash with rage.)

. . . Suppose he did all this, what then?

Bill Sikes. What then, by Gar! If he was left alive till I came, I'd grind his skull under the iron heel of my boot into as many grains as there are hairs upon his head.

Fagin. What if I did it? I, that know so much, and could hang so many besides myself!

Bill Sikes. I'd do something in the jail that 'ud get me put in irons; and if I was tried along with you, I'd fall upon you with them in the open court, and I'd beat out your brains afore the people. I should have such strength . . .

(He poises his brawny arm.)

. . . that I could smash your head as if a loaded wagon had gone over it.

Fagin. You would?

Bill Sikes. Would I? Try me!

Fagin. If it was Charley, or the Dodger, or Crackit, or . . .

Bill Sikes *(Impatiently).* I don't care who. Whoever it was, I'd serve them the same.

(Motioning Bill Sikes to be silent, **Fagin** *stoops over the bed on the floor and shakes* **Noah Claypole,** *to rouse him.)*

Fagin. Poor lad! He's tired . . . tired with watching for her, Bill.

Bill Sikes *(Drawing back).* Wot d'ye mean?

*(***Fagin** *bends over Noah Claypole again, and hauls him into a*

sitting posture. **Noah** *rubs his eyes, yawns, and looks sleepily about him.)*

Fagin *(To Noah Claypole).* Tell me that again . . .

(He points to Bill Sikes)

. . . Once again, just for him to hear.

Noah Claypole. Tell yer what?

Fagin. That about—NANCY . . .

(He clutches **Sikes** *by the wrist as if to prevent him leaving the house before he has heard enough.)*

. . . You followed her?

Noah Claypole. Yes.

Fagin. To London Bridge?

Noah Claypole. Yes.

Fagin. Where she met two people?

Noah Claypole. So she did.

Fagin. A gentleman and a lady? . . .

*(*Noah Claypole *nods.)*

. . . Who asked her to give up all her pals . . . and to tell where we do meet . . . and where it can best be watched from . . . and what time the people go there, which she did. She did all this. She told it all, every word, without a threat, without a murmur— she did—did she not?

Noah Claypole. That's right . . . That's just what it was!

Fagin. What did they say, about last Sunday?

Noah Claypole. About last Sunday? Why, I told yer that before.

Fagin. Again. Tell it again!

Noah Claypole. They asked her why she didn't come last Sunday, as she promised. She said she couldn't.

Fagin. Why—Why? Tell him that.

Noah Claypole. Because she was forcibly kept home by Bill, the man she was telling them of.

Bill Sikes. Hell's fire! . . . Let me go!

(He breaks fiercely from Fagin's grasp and rushes towards the door.)

Fagin. Bill! Bill! A word! Only a word!

Bill Sikes. Let me out! Don't speak to me; it's not safe. Let me out, I say!

Fagin. Hear me speak a word. You won't be . . . You won't be . . . too . . . violent, Bill? I mean, not too violent for safety. Be crafty, Bill, and not too bold.

(**Bill Sikes** *makes no reply, but rushes into the silent streets.*)

SCENE TEN
BILL SIKES' KEN

Oliver Twist. Without one pause, or moment's consideration; without turning his head to the right or left, or raising his eyes to the sky, or lowering them to the ground, but looking before him with savage resolution the robber held on his headlong course, nor muttered a word, nor relaxed a muscle, until he reached his own door. He opened it, softly, with a key; strode lightly up the stairs; entered his own room; double-locked the door, and, having lifted a heavy table against it, approached the bed.

Bill Sikes *(Rousing* **Nancy,** *who is lying there half-dressed).* Get up!

Nancy. It is you, Bill?

Bill Sikes. It is. Get up . . .

(He extinguishes the candle. **Nancy** *rises to undraw the curtain, but he thrusts his hand before her.)*

. . . Let it be. There's light enough for wot I've got to do.

Nancy. Bill! Why do you look like that at me? . . .

(He looks at her for a few seconds, with dilated nostrils and heaving breast; then, grasping her by the head and throat he drags her into the middle of the room, and, looking once towards the door, places his heavy hand upon her mouth.)

. . . Bill! Bill! I . . . I won't scream or cry . . . not once . . . hear me . . . speak to me . . . tell me what I have done!

Bill Sikes. You know, you she devil! . . . You were watched tonight; every word you said was heard.

Nancy. Then spare my life, for the love of Heaven, as I spared yours. Bill! Dear Bill! You cannot have the heart to kill me. Oh, think of all I have given up, only this one night, for you. You shall have time to think, and save yourself this crime; I will not loose my hold, you cannot throw me off. Bill, Bill, for dear God's sake, for your own, for mine, stop before you spill my blood! I have been true to you, upon my guilty soul I have! . . .

(He struggles violently to release his arms.)

. . . Bill! The gentleman, and that dear lady, told me tonight of a home in some foreign country where I could end my days in solitude and peace. Let me see them again, and beg them on my knees, to show the same mercy and goodness to you; and let us both leave this dreadful place, and far apart lead better lives, and forget how we have lived, except in prayers, and never see each other more. It is never too late to repent. They told me so . . . I feel it now . . . but we must have time . . . a little, little time!

(The housebreaker frees one arm, and grasps his pistol. The certainty of immediate detection, if he fires, flashes across his mind even in the midst of his fury; and he beats twice, with all the force he can summon, upon the upturned face that almost touches his own.)

Oliver. Nancy staggered and fell, nearly blinded with the blood that rained down from a deep gash in her forehead. Then she raised herself with difficulty upon her knees.

Nancy. Mercy, Lord, have mercy . . . .

Oliver. It was a ghastly figure to look upon. The murderer staggered backward to the wall, and shutting out the sight with his hand seized a heavy club and struck her down.

SCENE ELEVEN
A STREET CORNER

A Newsboy. Piper! Piper! Murder in Beffnal Green! Murder in Beffnal Green! Piper! Piper! . . .

(A customer approaches.)

. . . Piper, Sir? Thank you, Sir? Yes, Sir, foul murder in Beffnal Green, Sir. Woman found battered to death, Sir . . .

(He calls out again, as the customer moves away.)

. . . Piper! Piper! Big 'unt fer murderer! Big 'unt fer murderer! Piper! Piper! . . .

(Another customer approaches.)

. . . Piper, Sir? Thank you, Sir. Yes, Sir. 'Arf the country's 'unting fer 'im, Sir . . .

(He calls out again, as the customer moves away.)

. . . Piper! Piper! Reward offered in murder 'unt! Reward offered in murder 'unt! Piper! Piper! . . .

(A third customer approaches.)

. . . Piper, Sir? Thank you, Sir, Yussir, they think they've got 'im, Sir. In sarth-east Lunnon, Sir, dahn by the river, Sir. Got dogs arter 'im, an 'all. Wouldn't like to be 'im, nah. 'Ere, blow me pipers! I'm goinga see the fun!

SCENE TWELVE
THE KEN ON JACOB'S ISLAND

(A gloomy attic, in a ruinous house on a desolate island. **Toby Crackit** *is crouching by the window. He is accompanied by two of Fagin's confederates,* **Kags** *and* **Chitling***.)*

Toby Crackit. When was Fagin took, then?

Chitling. Just at dinner-time . . . two o'clock this arternoon. Charley and I made our lucky up the wash'us chimney, and Claypole got into the empty water-butt, 'ead downwards, but 'is legs was so precious long that they stuck out at the top, and so they took 'im too.

Toby Crackit. Wot's come of young Bates?

Chitling. 'E 'ung abaht, so as not to come over 'ere afore dark, but 'e'll be 'ere soon. There's nowhere else to go to, now. All the other kens is filled with traps.

Toby Crackit *(Biting his lips).* This is a smash! There's more than one will go with this.

Kags. The sessions is on. If they gets the inquest over, and that Claypole turns King's Evidence: as of course 'e will, from what 'e's said already: they can prove Fagin an accessory before the fact, and get the trial on on Friday, and he'll swing in six days from this, by God.

Chitling. You should 'ave 'eard the people groan. The officers fought like devils, or they'd 'ave torn 'im away. 'E was dahn once, but they made a ring round him, and fought their way along. You should have seen 'ow 'e looked abaht 'im, all muddy and bleeding, and clung . . .

(He stops speaking, and listens to a distant pattering noise.)

. . . What's that? . . .

(The three men peep through the window to the courtyard below.)

. . . It's Sikes' dog!

Toby Crackit. What's the meaning of this? 'E can't be coming 'ere! By Gar, we'll be took if 'e does.

Chitling. The cur looks 'arf blind.

Kags. And lame.

Chitling. 'E must 'ave come a long way.

Toby Crackit. Where can 'e 'ave come from? I reckon 'e's been to the other kens and found 'em full of strangers. That's why 'e's come on 'ere. But 'ow come 'e's 'ere without the other?

Chitling. The man can't 'ave made away with 'isself, do you think?

Kags. Nah. If 'e 'ad, the dog 'ud 'ave wanted ter stay wiv 'im. No. I think 'e's got out of the country and left the dog be'ind. 'E must 'ave given the brute the slip some'ow, or 'e wouldn't . . .

(There is a hurried knocking at the door below. All three men show their alarm in different ways.)

. . . 'Tis Young Bates!

(The knocking comes again.)

Toby Crackit. No, it's not 'im. Young Bates 'ud never knock like that. It's . . . it's the other. We must let 'im in.

Chitling. Ain't there any 'elp fer it?

Toby Crackit. None. 'E must come in.

*(Toby Crackit goes out. When he returns, he is followed by a man with the lower part of his face buried in a handkerchief. Blanched face, sunken eyes, hollow cheeks, beard of three days' growth, wasted flesh– it is the very ghost of Bill Sikes. **Sikes** looks from one to another in silence. If an eye is furtively raised and meets his, it is instantly averted.)*

Bill Sikes *(At last)*. I've 'eard that Fagin's took. Is it true, or a lie?

Toby Crackit. True.

(The men are silent again.)

Bill Sikes. Damn you all! Have you nothing to say to me? . . .

(There is an uneasy movement, but nobody speaks.)

. . . You that keep this house . . .

(He turns his face to Toby Crackit.)

. . . Do you mean to sell me, or to let me lie here till this hunt is over?

Toby Crackit *(After some hesitation)*. You may stop 'ere if yer think it safe.

Bill Sikes. Is . . . it . . . the body . . . is it buried? . . .

(The men shake their heads.)

. . . Why isn't it? Wot do they keep such ugly things above the ground for? . . .

(There is a knock at the door.)

. . . Who's that knocking?

*(Toby Crackit goes to see, and returns with **Charley Bates**.)*

Charley Bates *(Seeing Bill Sikes, and drawing back)*. Toby! Why didn't yer tell me this, downstairs? . . .

*(**Bill Sikes** advances, as if he wishes to shake hands with the boy.)*

. . . Let me go!

Bill Sikes. Charley! Don't yer . . . Don't yer know me?

Charley Bates. Don't come nearer me! You monster! . . .

*(The murderer and the boy look at each other. Then **Bill Sikes'** eyes sink gradually to the ground.)*

. . . Witness you three—I'm not afraid of 'im . . . If they come here after 'im, I'll give 'im up, I will. I tell you out at once. 'E may kill me fer it if 'e likes, or if 'e dares, but if I am 'ere I'll give 'im up . . . Murder! 'Elp! . . .

(He dashes to the window)

. . . Murder! 'Elp! If there's the pluck of a man among you three, you'll 'elp me. Murder! 'Elp! Down wiv 'im! . . .

*(**Charley Bates** flings himself at Bill Sikes. The two roll on the ground in a desperate struggle, the boy never ceasing to call for help with all his might. **Bill Sikes** has Young Bates down, with his knee on the boy's throat, when **Toby Crackit** pulls him back with a look of alarm and points to the window. There are lights gleaming below, voices in loud and earnest conversation, the tramp of hurried footsteps crossing the nearest wooden bridge. Then comes a loud knocking at the door.)*

. . . 'Elp! 'E's 'ere! 'E's 'ere! Break down the door!

Voices outside. In the King's name!

Charley Bates. Break down the door! They'll never open it . . . Break down the door!

(Strokes, thick and heavy, rattle upon the door and window shutters.)

Bill Sikes. That door! Quick!

(He seizes Charley Bates, and drags him out, kicking and struggling. Then he returns, having bolted the boy away.)

. . . Is the downstairs door fast?

Toby Crackit. Double-locked and chained.

Bill Sikes. The panels . . . Are they strong?

Toby Crackit. Lined with sheet-iron.

Bill Sikes. And the winders, too?

Toby Crackit. Yus, and the winders.

Bill Sikes *(Going to the window and menacing the crowd).* Do yer worst! I'll cheat yer yet! . . .

(There are cries from the infuriated throng outside: 'Set the house on fire!' 'Shoot him!' 'Twenty guineas to the man who brings a ladder!')

. . . Give me a rope. A long rope. They're all in front. I may drop inter Folly Ditch, and clear off that way. Give me a rope, or I shall do three more murders.

(Toby Crackit produces a long, strong cord. Bill Sikes takes it, and goes out to a window at the back of the house.)

The Crowd: He's out on the roof! He's out at the back! Come on!

Toby Crackit. 'E's gone out of that little winder on to the roof. Come 'ere. Crouch dahn. You can see 'im through this . . .

(The three men crouch down.)

. . . Look! 'E's tying a noose in the rope. 'E's going to tie the other end rahnd the chimney stack, I tell yer.

Chitling. No, 'e ain't.

Toby Crackit. What's 'e going to tie it rahnd, then? There you are! What did I tell yer? 'E 'as. Nah, 'e's goin' ter let hisself dahn . . .

(Cries of 'Keep back!' 'He's going to jump for it!')

. . . 'E's slipped! Chrisalmighty, 'e's slipped!

(There is an unearthly screech from outside as Bill Sikes falls thirty five feet.)

. . . 'E's 'anged 'isself! Oh, Gor, the poor creetur! 'E's gone and 'anged 'isself.

Chitling. What 'ad we better do now?

Toby Crackit. We'd better scarper quick. We can git away, mebbe, if we makes a dash while they're a-thinking of cutting 'im dahn. C'mon. 'Urry.

(The three men make off, leaving Charley Bates to call to the people to let him out.)

SCENE THIRTEEN
A PRIVATE ROOM IN AN
HOTEL NEAR THE WORKHOUSE

(Mr. Brownlow leads two sturdy men into the room. These men are escorting Monks, who has been brought there under duress. At the rear of the procession we see Mr. Grimwig and Young Oliver.)

Mr. Brownlow. He knows the alternative. If he hesitates, or moves a finger but as you bid him, drag him into the street, call for the aid of the police, and impeach him as a felon in my name.

Monks. How dare you do this to me? By what authority am I kidnapped in the street and brought here by these dogs?

Mr. Brownlow. By mine. Those persons are indemnified by me. If you complain of being deprived of your liberty, throw yourself for protection on the law. I will appeal to the law, too; but when you have gone too far to recede, do not sue to me for leniency, for then the power will have passed into other hands . . .

(Monks hesitates.)

. . . You will decide quickly if you wish me to prefer my charges publicly, and consign you to dire punishment. If not, if you appeal to my forbearance, and the mercy of those you have deeply injured, seat yourself, without a word, in that chair. It has waited for you for long enough . . .

(Monks mutters some unintelligible words.)

. . . You will be prompt. A word from me, and the alternative has gone for ever . . .

(Still Monks hesitates.)

. . . I have not the inclination to parley, and as I advocate the dearest interests of others, I have not the right.

Monks. Is there . . . is there . . . no middle course?

Mr. Brownlow. None . . .

(Monks reads in Mr. Brownlow's countenance nothing but severity and determination, so he shrugs his shoulders and sits down. Mr. Brownlow turns to the attendants.)

. . . Please wait outside, and come if I ring.

81

(The attendants go out.)

Monks. This is pretty treatment, sir, from my father's oldest friend.

Mr. Brownlow. It is a painful task, but these declarations which have been made in London before many gentlemen must be in substance repeated here.

Mr. Monks. Go on. Quick. I have almost done enough, I think. Don't keep me here.

Mr. Brownlow. This child . . .

(He draws **Young Oliver** *to him, and lays his hand upon his head)*

. . . Whom I intend to adopt herewith as my own son, is your half brother, the illegitimate son of your father, my dear friend Edwin Leeford, by poor young Agnes Fleming, who died in giving him birth.

Monks. Must I be forced to listen to this?

Mr. Brownlow. When your father died, so suddenly and tragically, he left on his desk two papers. One was a letter to this Agnes. The second was his will.

Monks. I have nothing to disclose. Talk on, if you must.

Mr. Brownlow. Your mother did what she considered to be her duty. She destroyed the will, leaving the secret, and the gain, to you at her own death. It contained a reference to some child likely to be the result of his sad connection. This child was accidentally encountered by you, and your suspicions were first awakened by his resemblance to his father. You repaired to the place of his birth. There existed proofs—proofs long suppressed—of his birth and parentage. Those proofs were destroyed by you, and now, in your own words to your accomplice the Jew, '*the only proofs of the boy's identity lie at the bottom of the river, and the old hag that received them from the mother is rotting in her coffin.*' Unworthy son, coward, liar—you, who hold your councils with thieves and murderers in dark rooms at night—you, Edward Leeford, do you still brave me?

Monks. No! No! No!

Mr. Brownlow. Then you will tell us, no doubt, what happened to Agnes' locket, and ring?

Monks. I bought them from a vile old woman at the workhouse, who stole them from the nurse, who stole them from the corpse. You know what became of them.

(Mr. Brownlow nods to Mr. Grimwig, who disappears with great alacrity, and shortly returns pushing in Mrs. Bumble, and dragging her unwilling consort after him.)

Mr. Bumble. Do my hi's deceive me? Or is that little Oliver? Oh, O—li—ver, if you know'd how I've been a-grieving for you—

Mrs. Bumble. Hold your tongue, fool.

Mr. Grimwig *(Tartly)*. Come, Sir. Suppress your feelings.

Mr. Bumble. I will do my endeavours, Sir . . .

(He turns to Mr. Brownlow.)

. . . How do you do, Sir? I hope you are very well?

Mr. Brownlow *(Pointing to Monks)*. Do you know that person?

Mrs. Bumble. No.

Mr. Brownlow *(To Mr. Bumble)*. Perhaps you don't?

Mr. Bumble. I never saw him in all my life.

Mr. Brownlow. Nor sold him anything, perhaps?

Mrs. Bumble. No.

Mr. Brownlow. You never had, perhaps a certain gold locket and ring?

Mrs. Bumble. Certainly not! Why are we brought here to answer such nonsense as this?

(Again Mr. Brownlow nods to Mr. Grimwig. This time, Mr. Grimwig produces the two workhouse females who watched over Old Sally's deathbed.)

The Female Pauper. You sent us away, the night Old Sally died, but our ears is long, old as we be.

The Old Woman *(Looking round, and wagging her toothless jaws.)* Ay, ay!

The Female Pauper. We heard her try to tell you what she'd done, and saw you take a paper from her hand, and watched you, too, next day, to the pawnbroker's shop.

The Old Woman. Yes, and it was a locket and gold ring. We saw it given you. We were by. Oh! We were by.

Mr. Grimwig *(To Mrs. Bumble, with a motion towards the door.)* Would you like to see the pawnbroker himself?

Mrs. Bumble. No. If he . . .

(She points to Monks.)

... has been coward enough to confess, as I see he has, I have nothing more to say. I did sell them. What of that?

Mr. Brownlow. Nothing. Except that it remains for us to take care that neither of you is employed in a situation of trust again. You may leave the room.

Mr. Bumble *(Looking round with great ruefulness as* **Mr. Grimwig** *disappears with the three women).* I hope that this unfortunate little circumstance will not deprive me of my porochial office?

Mr. Brownlow. Indeed it will. You may make up your mind to that, and think yourself well off besides.

Mr. Bumble. It was all Mrs. Bumble. She would do it.

Mr. Brownlow. That is no excuse. You were a party to the destruction of these trinkets, and indeed are the more guilty of the two, in the eye of the law, for the law supposes that your wife acts under your direction.

Mr. Bumble *(Squeezing his hat).* If the law supposes that, the law is a hass ... the law is a hidiot. If that's the eye of the law, the law is a bachelor; and the worst I wish the law is, that his eye may be opened by experience—by experience.

*(*Mr. Bumble *fixes his hat on very tight, and goes out.)*

Mr. Brownlow. And now, Oliver my son, we have one more duty to perform before we can say that justice has truly been carried out. It will not be a pleasant one, but ...

*(*Mr. Grimwig *returns, and signals to Mr. Brownlow.)*

... My boy, our carriage awaits.

*(*Mr. Brownlow *leads* Oliver *affectionately out. The sturdy men, bidden by* Mr. Grimwig, *remove* Monks.)*

SCENE FOURTEEN
THE CONDEMNED CELL AT NEWGATE

*(*Mr. Brownlow *presents an order of admission to the prisoner. He is accompanied by* Young Oliver.)*

The Chief Warder. Is the young gentleman to come too, Sir? It's not a sight for children, Sir.

Mr. Brownlow. It is not indeed, my friend; but my business with this man is intimately connected with him; and as this child has seen him in the full career of his success and villainy, I think it as well—even at the cost of some pain and fear—that he should see him now.

(The Chief Warder touches his hat and leads the visitors towards the cells.)

The Chief Warder *(Pausing on the way).* This is the place he will pass through, Sir, when the clock strikes eight. If you step this way, you can see the door he goes out at.

Mr. Brownlow. And what is that noise?

The Chief Warder. They're just a-putting the finishing touches to the scaffold, Sir. The crowd's been growing since midnight.

(They pass into the Condemned Cell. **Fagin** *is seated on his bed, rocking himself from side to side, with a countenance more like that of a snared beast than the face of a man.)*

Fagin *(Mumbling to himself).* Good boy, Charley . . . Well done . . . Oliver, too, ha! ha! ha! Oliver, too ; . . quite the gentleman now . . . quite the . . . take that boy away to bed . . . Take him away! . . . Do you hear me, some of you?

The Chief Warder. Fagin!

Fagin. That's me! An old man, my Lord; a very old, old man.

The Chief Warder. Here . . . Here's somebody wants to see you, to ask you some questions, I suppose. Fagin! Fagin! Are you a man?

Fagin *(Looking up with a face retaining no human expression but rage and terror).* I shan't be one long. Strike them all dead! What right have they to butcher me? . . .

(He catches sight of Young Oliver and Mr. Brownlow and shrinks to the furthest corner of the seat.)

. . . What do you want? Ah! Ah! What do you want?

The Chief Warder *(Holding Fagin down).* Steady! . . .

(He turns to Mr. Brownlow.)

. . . Now, Sir, tell him what you want. Quick, if you please, for he grows worse as the time comes closer.

Mr. Brownlow *(Advancing).* You have some papers, which were placed in your hands, for better security, by a man called Monks.

85

Fagin. It's a lie together. I haven't one—not one.

Mr. Brownlow. For the love of Goodness, do not say that now, upon the very verge of death; but tell me where they are. You know that Sikes is dead; that Monks has confessed; that there is no hope of any further gain. Where are those papers?

Fagin *(Beckoning to Young Oliver).* Oliver! Here, here! Let me whisper to you.

Young Oliver *(Relinquishing Mr. Brownlow's hand).* I am not afraid.

Fagin *(Drawing Young Oliver towards him).* The papers are in a canvas bag, in a hole a little way up the chimney in the top front-room. I want to talk to you, my dear. I want to talk to you.

Young Oliver. Yes, yes. Let me say a prayer. Do! Let me say one prayer. Say only one, upon your knees with me, and we will talk till morning.

Fagin *(Pushing Young Oliver before him towards the door).* Outside, outside. Say I've gone to sleep—they'll believe you. You can get me out, if you take me so. Now then, now then!

Young Oliver. Oh! God forgive this wretched man!

Fagin. That's right, that's right. That'll help us on. This door first. If I shake and tremble, as we pass the gallows, don't you mind, but hurry on. Now, now, now!

The Chief Warder. Have you nothing else to ask him, Sir?

Mr. Brownlow. No other question. If I hoped we could recall him to a sense of his position . . .

The Chief Warder *(Shaking his head).* Nothing will do that, Sir. You had better leave him.

(Warders appear.)

Fagin. Press on. Press on. Softly, but not too slow. Faster! Faster!

*(The warders disengage **Young Oliver** from **Fagin**'s grasp. **Fagin** sends up cry after cry as **Mr. Brownlow** leads **Young Oliver** from the cell. Then Newgate Bell starts to toll, and the warders bow their heads. On the eighth stroke, **the Hangman** and his assistants enter the cell. They pinion **Fagin**, and take him out to the scaffold.)*

86

Selected Titles
Dramascripts

(Series editor, Guy Williams)

selected titles

Topical plays

Adam's Ark
Harold Hodgeson
0-17-432364-6

Carrigan Street
John Pick
0-17-432365-4

Frankly Frankie
Rony Robinson
0-17-432366-2

Hijack
Charles Wells
0-17-432367-0

The Terrible Fate of Humpty Dumpty
David Calcutt
0-17-432369-7

Unman, Wittering and Zygo
Giles Cooper
0-17-432370-0

Adaptations of Classics

Macbeth
William Shakespeare
0-17-432363-8

Romeo and Juliet
William Shakespeare
0-17-432371-9

Twelfth Night
William Shakespeare
0-17-432373-5

Julius Caesar
William Shakespeare
0-17-432374-3

The Tempest
William Shakespeare
0-17-432376-X

The Merchant of Venice
William Shakespeare
0-17-432378-6

A Midsummer Night's Dream
William Shakespeare
0-17-432379-4

Plays from other sources

The Machine Gunners
Robert Westall
0-17-432380-8

The Doctor and the Devils
Dylan Thomas
0-17-432382-4

The Government Inspector
Nicolai Gogol
0-17-432383-2

A Christmas Carol
Charles Dickens
0-17-432385-9

The Rocking Horse Winner
D H Lawrence
0-17-432386-7

Winter Plays
Guy Williams
0-17-432344-1